DUSK IN THE FROG POND

and other stories

D1715470

DUSK IN THE FROG POND

FROG POND

and other stories

Rummana Chowdhury

INANNA poetry & fiction

Toronto, Ontario, Canada
www.inanna.ca

We gratefully acknowledge the support of the Canada Council for the Arts and the Ontario Arts Council for our publishing program. We also acknowledge the financial support of the Government of Canada.

Dusk in the Frog Pond is a work of fiction. All the characters portrayed in this book are fictitious and any resemblance to persons living or dead is purely coincidental.

Cover design: Val Fullard

Library and Archives Canada Cataloguing in Publication

Title: Dusk in the frog pond : and other stories / Rummana Chowdhury.
Names: Chowdhury, Rummana, author.
Identifiers: Canadiana (print) 20210361417 | Canadiana (ebook)
20210361433 | ISBN 9781771337977
    (softcover) | ISBN 9781771337984 (HTML) | ISBN 9781771337991
(PDF)
Classification: LCC PS8605.H69 D87 2021 | DDC C813/.6—dc23
Printed and Bound in Canada.

Published in Canada by
Inanna Publications and Education Inc.
210 Founders College, York University
4700 Keele Street, Toronto, Ontario M3J 1P3
Telephone: (416) 736-5356 Fax: (416) 736-5765
Email: inanna.publications@inanna.ca Website: www.inanna.ca

*For my beloved daughter **Fariah**,*
Who was our inspiration and wisdom, like the enchantment of
unwritten poetry…
Her life was devoted to being the Voice for the Voiceless. She was only
thirty-five years old, pregnant with her unborn child of thirty-six weeks,
when the mystery of death befell them…
Her footprints will be eternal, like the lingering fragrance in our souls…

Contents

1   Rodela's Invisible Colours

9   She Is / She Isn't

16   Dusk in the Frog Pond

31   Monsoon Breeze

38   Shadow Over the Henna Tree

45   The Door Remains Closed

55   Her Pink Pearls

65   Of Fox and Fiddle

77   *Acknowledgements*

RODELA'S INVISIBLE COLOURS

Rodela clutched her shawl tightly around her neck and shoulders, an irritating cough persisting at the bottom of her throat. Kolkata should have been warmer this time of year; it usually was, but then again, she should have been more prepared. The doctor warned her before she left that her body would not recover from another bout of pneumonia. So, here is the truth of aging, the slow decline of one's ability to recover, the reality that something as seemingly simple as underestimating the windchill on a walk to your destination could mean the end of you. She wondered if coming to Kolkata to shop was a mistake, wondered if she was too old, too tired for the various tasks she'd set out for herself. There were the saris, at least seven, she'd promised to buy for friends and family. Saris here were a third of the price they were back home in Toronto. She had no time nor occasion to wear more of her own, but shopping for others was a pleasure, however tiresome at times. Rodela loved sifting through the shops, thinking of the colours and patterns that would go over best.

She ducked into a store that seemed a little brighter, a little more inviting than the rest. There were streets in Kolkata seemingly reserved for saris alone, and she'd positioned herself in the centre of Sudder Street, the best one. From outside, the scent of fresh street food still lingered. Her West Bengali friends back home had told her to avoid the fancy restaurants, which were designed to draw tourists and whose food suffered for it, and to stick to the street food. She'd followed their advice and had not been disappointed. She'd indulged first in kurtis, the dahi barah with chaat masala and tamarind still lingering on her tongue. Masala coffee beat the food though. Each night before bed, she had a cup downstairs in the hotel, then slept the deepest, most contented sleep of her life.

The shawl Rodela wore had been snuck into her suitcase last minute by her sister, who had warned her about the cold. The scent of her sister's Modern Muse perfume still lingered, and Rodela couldn't help but think fondly of her sister who had a habit of saving her, of bringing comfort when Rodela was unable to comfort herself. There was the name too, Modern Muse, with the scent, and with the recollection of that name came the recollection of the first and only time Rodela had been called a muse. It was ten years into her marriage, when a friend, a poet by the name of Ayaan, leaned in on a crowded sidewalk on a sunny day and whispered in her ear, "You're my muse." She delighted in the idea that she could have had something to do with her friend's work. Rodela loved poetry. She loved poets. "*Kabbolakhkhi*, I was his artistic inspiration," she proudly whispered.

The memory lingered as she walked further into the store, now smiling a little, looking forward to her task. She fell in love with the first kurti that the salesman showed her. It was a deep coffee-coloured material with tiny white jui flowers delicately embroidered throughout. The salesman was patient and showed her one sari after another, pulling each down off the shelf with the same care he had the previous. They looked at dozens together, and at the end, Rodela came back to the first.

"I have seen it many times," the salesman said, "women often come back to their first choice."

Rodela looked up at him. Did she imagine faint laughter behind his soft voice? "It is just the size. I am a size bigger, but you said this was your largest size."

"I think this size is perfect for you, Mem Saheb, but if anything is wrong or if it does not fit you, then bring it back. I will gladly exchange it."

"I know you will, but the problem is that I do not have much time on this trip."

"Mem Saheb, just take the ones you like. Go back to your hotel, don't pay me any money now, try them on and if you are satisfied, then pay me tomorrow on your way out of the city."

Rodela looked up into his twinkling eyes and salt-and-pepper moustache above his smiling lips. "I will be taking at least four of them and matching tights. That will be around two thousand rupees!"

"That is not a problem. Should I pack them?"

Now Rodela was a little incredulous and agitated. "But you do not even know me. I am from Bangladesh, and I will be leaving Kolkata after three days."

The middle-aged salesman started packing her things and firmly told her, "I have been selling to customers for over forty years now, and I know my money is not going anywhere."

Rodela did not have energy to protest. She silently and gratefully took the shopping bag. How could he give her this clothing without any deposit or assurance she'd return? He did not ask the name of her hotel or room number or even her name.

The kurtis fit her perfectly and she was anxious the next day to make her payment. Her faith in humanity advanced a little. She was in disbelief that an unknown shopkeeper would have so much trust in her; this would never happen in Canada.

Rodela's first week back in Toronto was difficult. She had not cooked, cleaned, or done grocery shopping for over thirty days. Now that she was back, getting up at 5:30 a.m. to catch the subway to work seemed intolerable. She sorely missed her nightly body massages in Bangladesh by the maid Arzu and the dal puris and parathas she'd had for breakfast. She also tried not to remember her siblings', nieces', nephews' and aunts' and uncles' love and hospitality. The refreshingly sweet, sultry breeze in the month of Falgun haunted her. She ached to return.

Here, her husband Khalid and sons were engrossed in their own lives, and she once again felt isolated. Where did it all begin, and where did it end? Was there any kind of meaning in her life? What was the purpose of uninterrupted days and nights of monotonous activities? What was the purpose of all this in the end?

A few weeks after her return to Toronto, still nursing her sorrow, Rodela met her friend Ayaan by chance, while picnicking with her boys by the shore of Lake Ontario. The boys were dipping their feet in the cool blue water of the lake and eating popcorn with the loudly barking seagulls. Her husband was golfing with his office buddies, as was his newest habit on weekends. The boundless sky was smiling its blue and white clouds. She walked towards her favourite spot amidst the rocks where strong waves lashed out.

"And what is on my angel's mind?" Ayaan came from behind and embraced her.

She felt his sudden hardness and disentangled herself. "Where have you been the last few months?" she asked, keeping her distance.

"In the deepest core of your heart, where I belong."

"You never answered my emails or text messages, and now you behave as if nothing happened?"

"Did anything happen, my angel? I am still where I always was."

"You never even picked up the phone once to call me."

"You are always in my heart. I have spoken to you."

"Only when I called you. Then you are the most cordial person in the world. You never call me on your own."

"My very own angel."

Rodela couldn't help but cry.

He touched a tear, wiped it off her face, and smiled. "It's fine. It's all perfectly fine," he said.

She watched as he walked the shore and out of sight, then returned to her sons who'd been too occupied with their snacks and some ongoing spat about the art of hole digging to notice their mother's absence, let alone her encounter.

It was another month before Rodela and Ayaan met again. Of course, she hadn't been trying to see him, wouldn't have planned it, but if she was honest with herself, thoughts of him kept creeping in. Her husband, who had been so ravenous when they were first married, barely touched her nor spoke a word that wasn't strictly pragmatic. She missed the way it had been but saw no way to return to it. So, on long nights, lying next to her sleeping husband, Rodela let her thoughts wander to the way she felt for her old friend. There was more to this than her husband's distance, his denial of her. There was the increasing independence of her sons, who were in high school now and who wanted as much distance from their mother as they could get. She felt unwanted, unneeded, undesired. Often, on the CBC, she'd heard stories about the declining state of the country. Were things really that bad, or was it a reflection of her own inner state? It was 2008, and the market had plummeted, instances of terrorism and suicide were up, mental health issues were on the rise, divorce became the norm. Her emotions seemed to be on a rollercoaster ride too these days.

In spite of all of this, Rodela allowed herself to be happy when she saw her old friend at a gathering of Dhaka University alumni across town. She smelled him before she saw him. It was as if, with the introduction of that single scent, all the world lit up for the first time in months.

He came into view and quickly approached. "What's up, angel?"

"It's only been thirty days, what new thing could have happened?" She couldn't help her smugness, though in truth she thought the world had stopped for her in the last few months. Every second, every minute, every hour of those days had felt unmanageably infinite. There were no emails, no text messages, no phone calls, altogether no contact or communication from Ayaan.

How could a person who had once, in one of his serious moments, proclaimed unending love for her be so careless, nonchalant and hurtful? If she asked him, he would just say that she was always reigning in his heart. She did not want to listen to the same artificial answer again and again. She had to accept the reality that he no longer cared for her. Better late than never.

She thought of the day they'd met, many years ago, in Dundas Square, where the Bengali Cultural Society was celebrating a Bangla festival. Rodela had been asked to sing a selection of Nazrul Geeti songs to kick off the event. She was a trained singer, though in her adult life there were fewer and fewer opportunities to showcase her talent. Nazrul was the national poet of Bangladesh. He was not only a rebel poet, but also a great political, social, cultural, literary and intellectual genius for both East and West Bengal. Now he had gained global recognition for his work.

Rodela sang with wholehearted devotion to the material, savouring every minute of her chance to pay respect to a poet she so admired. She wore a red-and-white silk sari with fresh white flowers in her braids. She knew she'd performed well and felt unshakable in both talent and appearance. She wished Khalid had been there to revel with her in this moment, to see her in her prime. But it wasn't unusual at all these days for her to be alone.

She stepped off the stage and nearly into the arms of one of the most handsome men she'd seen that night.

"May I compliment you on your singing?" the man said. Rodela looked up into the eyes of the stranger.

He was gazing so intently at her that all at once she felt very shy. His eyes were like pools of endless warmth and intellect. They made her breathless.

"Do you also sing?" she said at last.

"No, I wish the Almighty had given me such talent. I would have nothing more to ask from Him."

"I am sure He has given you other qualities."

The stranger introduced himself as Ayaan, a software engineer living in Canada for over thirty-five years.

"I often go to Dhaka University concerts, and I have heard your singing many times."

Rodela was taken aback. Had she met him in Bangladesh?

He told her he was a writer, that he was quite prolific back home.

"I go to the Ekushey Book Fair every year in Bangladesh, upon my publisher's invitation, for the launching of my books," he humbly said.

"I think I have watched your interviews from the Bangla Academy premises through Channel i and NTV."

"Do you also write?"

"Not as much as you, just a couple of poetry books."

He laughed, "A singer and a poet! Am I in luck today!"

They sat down to coffee and jhaalmoori, spicy puffed rice with lots of green peppers and fresh coriander. There was magic in the air amidst the many stalls of handmade bags, saris and bangles from Bangladesh.

Rodela was surprised by her own arousal. She let the stranger kiss her, not once but several times. She felt alive.

The months that followed were like a kaleidoscope. They fell head over heels in love with each other. It was just like a storybook. They could not see, hear, talk, make love to each other enough. Their time together flew by with the speed of a Concorde jet. Then, one day, Rodela felt his disentanglement and aloofness.

She could not understand where she had gone wrong. As the summer turned to fall and winter, the emerald leaves of her heart turned grey. The boundless sky, the dancing waves of the sea, the twinkling stars in the Milky Way — everything induced within her pathos and sadness. For her, it was falling in love again. For him, she was only a part-time pleasure. He had used all his soft persuasions, intellectual abilities and womanizing expertise to conquer her heart.

They met again at a mutual friend's dinner. Khalid had accompanied her because they had some friends in common, and he probably had nothing better to do. Ayaan and his wife were seated opposite to them at the dinner table. He had never spoken about his wife, so she had presumed he was single. Rodela felt Ayaan's touch on her thighs. She moved away. How could a person switch on and off in this manner? She felt his gaze on her but avoided his eyes. She was teaching herself to forget. Every step of the way was very painful.

She played a game with herself where in her own private world there was no second person in her life. There was no Khalid or Ayaan. There was no one. She had to adapt to the fact that no one loved her anymore and that she loved no one. She was climbing the initial steps to a kingdom where she would be the only living person left.

Living without love, without being loved, would be a long, hard path. The stars twinkling above were trying to tell her that the sun and the moon also lead solitary lives with no companions. She had to live for herself for today, and for the days to come.

SHE IS / SHE ISN'T

Mou didn't recognize herself. Reflected in mirrors and shop windows throughout New York was a put-together woman in the prime of her life: handsome, upright, composed. It was a lie, a physical composition that rebelled against the true state of things, that shielded it so well no one would think to stop, to ask if this woman was okay. This woman was not okay. Her heart fluttered, her blood pressure rose and her eyes burned at random intervals throughout the day, sparked by one or another pang of regret, of the ever-present questions: *how did I get here? How can I get out?*

She did not choose her husband. He was chosen for her. She did not choose to move to New York. New York was chosen for her. Back in Dhaka, almost a year ago, she'd been student, twenty-two and carefree, applying for her Master's in Civic Studies, poring over college catalogues and excitedly discussing her prospects with friends in the warm belly of a public park. When she'd arrived home, out of the blue, her parents sat her down and presented her with the prospect of a husband. She hadn't seen it coming, sat perched on the edge of her seat at the kitchen table with her parents side-by-side across from her. The sun was bright through the window; there was the sound of birds. Mou froze. She wanted to run away from this moment, erase it. She could no longer see the sun nor hear the birds. All there was now was the deafening sound of her own protestations, both in her mind and in audible bursts. She thought back now on what her parents had said.

"He lives in America, in New York. He has a job. He is here to see his mother, then will return to New York in two days. You must commit now or the opportunity will be lost."

"What opportunity?" she'd asked. "I have everything I want here."

"America," they'd said. Just… America.

Mou wondered if she'd asked her parents what sort of job the man had. What sort of home. She thought she did. She might not have. So many things were difficult to say to one's parents back home. She asked his name. They told her it was Matin. She cried a little. Knew there was no choice here, not really. She felt the pull of a well-planned destiny, and in the face of it, knew she was impotent.

Mou and Matin met formally at a handicraft shop halfway between their houses. Mou was accompanied by her mother and Matin by his aunt, who had first delivered the proposal to the family the day before. Matin was handsome enough, a little taller than Mou, with a rustic, faraway look to him. He was stoic and well-mannered, smelled of mints and some sort of citrus. Mou wondered if he found her attractive. He must have. He'd seen her before proposing, in a photograph, anyways. She asked herself if she found him attractive. She could learn to.

The wedding commenced without delay, and no matter how hard Mou searched for an opportunity to protest, she never found one. Soon she was a wife. She had a husband. Soon that husband was on a plane back to New York, and within the month a visa and plane ticket arrived so she could follow. Everything had happened so fast. She said goodbye to her friends from college, tried her best to be optimistic, looking up pictures of New York that might spark her enthusiasm, imagining herself living in a little brownstone next to the park, a short walk to college. She imagined her new American friends, her new American manner. It was exciting in a way. There was potential, mystery. She could not say it would be good, but she couldn't say it would be bad either.

Matin rented a small apartment in Jackson Heights, a one-bedroom with the kitchen just to one side of the small living room, one small window above the sink. Matin worked two jobs during the day and drove a taxi at night. It was as she'd suspected: the man had nothing. She would have even less. Through a few tired conversations on the hours she could steal with him, Matin had revealed to her that it hadn't been his will to get married. His dying mother had summoned him over to marry. It was her dying wish, and it was a wish that had taken more resources than Matin had. Mou sat on the small, low, blue couch in the living room and considered her situation. She had sympathy for Matin, of course, but what of herself? There was nothing for her here but solitude in some tight, tucked-away apartment.

She told herself she could bear being away from her friends and the warm sun of Bangladesh so long as she had the opportunity to study. That was all that really mattered. That was what would open for her the doors that weren't open to her husband. She could pull them out of this with time.

Mou prepared a special supper for Matin on the weekend and rouged her cheeks, wore her kindest smile. Matin looked worn, distant. She knew she'd need to cut through that if she was to broach the subject of her education.

She leaned over and squeezed his leg, kissed his mouth.

"How are you settling in, my dear?" Matin said, not quite making eye contact.

"Okay, I think. I understand the neighbourhood now, know my way around the subway and to the market. I've been looking at the schools too, at NYU and Columbia. Some of the smaller colleges just in case, but I think my grades will carry me for here."

"What are you talking about?"

Mou laughed, "About going to school to get my Master's degree, silly. Enrolment is next month, and I need to make up my mind soon about where to apply."

Matin's head lowered, his brow furrowed. He stood and walked to a small filing cabinet at the side of the fridge. He came back with a beige file folder and opened it in front of Mou.

"What is this?"

"This," Matin said, pointing at a page of numbers, "is the line of credit I had to take out to get you here. I am thirty thousand dollars in debt. Rent is sixteen hundred. There is no way, I'm afraid, that I can even begin to think about putting you through school."

Mou was undeterred. "I can work."

"No," Matin said with a traditional and quite ancient seeming authority, "you need to focus on the home, on getting acquainted with North American ways of life. There are free language courses, and lots of opportunities for community involvement. Put your energy there. I will not have my wife working."

"But…"

"I said no."

Mou retreated into herself. There was nothing now to be optimistic about. She noticed every crack in the wall, each small roach that scurried through the kitchen at night when the light was dim, the leaking tap, the loudly walking upstairs neighbours. Everything irked her, hurt even. She was alone here and with no prospects. How could this get better? How could this be anything but a lifelong drudge?

The next morning, at 6 a.m., when Matin left for work, Mou walked alone down to the Hudson River. There were few people out at that hour, and she felt a little calm happiness settle as she was reminded of the Karnaphuli River back home where sweet breezes would run through her hair on aimless afternoons with friends. She thought of the picnics and outdoor concerts, of the heated but friendly political debates late into the hot evenings, of the barefoot silent procession of the Shahid Minar or Martyrs' Memorial, the Ekushey Book Fair and Roadside Dramas at the Shilpakala Academy. It was all behind her now, all out of reach, and what was in its place? What had she to enjoy here all by herself?

Pining soon died down, as did regret. Mou settled into the numb pattern of the day-to-day — washing, cooking, sleeping. She no longer listened to music or went out to movies, sought out no new friends or community activities. She sat and worked and stared without thought through the small window, watching the season slowly shift to winter. The leaves were dead now. The air was cold. Mou went cold as well.

The change came in the dead of winter. Matin had run into a childhood friend named Probal during his lunch break by a food truck. Probal had migrated to New York around the same time Matin had, and while they'd been in contact then, Matin's busy schedule had caused them to drift apart. Probal reintroduced himself into Matin's, and then Mou's, life with vigour, a vigour Mou found uplifting, intoxicating even.

Here's the thing. Mou didn't want her marriage and neither did Matin. He did it to satisfy his dying mother. She did it for her parents, who'd been raised to believe a daughter of marrying age must be married. According to Islamic Shari'ah, to deny marriage past that age would be a sin that Allah would hold them responsible for, letting their daughter wait, letting her do what was called Free Mixing — or marrying by choice, for love. They were victims of circumstance and could not find their own happiness within it.

It was when Probal began renting out the couch in the living room that all began to dissolve. Mou believed in marriage, in its sanctity. She believed in the will of Allah, but she couldn't understand why that will would want her to be so miserable. It was hard not to watch Probal as he moved through the apartment. He was virile and graceful, tall, broad and handsome. He had an ease that Mou envied, that she wanted to be close to. Next to Probal, Matin seemed to fade into almost nothing.

It was Probal's first night on the couch. Mou couldn't sleep. There was an urgent energy that kept her tossing and turning next to her snoring husband. She could have kicked him, and he wouldn't have budged. From the living room she heard a little hum, a rhythm that slowly became clearer the longer she focused on it. It was a song by Jagjit Singh, and it seemed to get louder the longer she lay there listening. Soon she couldn't help herself. She got up slowly, leaving the husband she barely knew snoring on the bed, and walked in her translucent white nightgown towards the kitchen.

She felt her way through the darkness and opened the refrigerator, letting it cast its pale blue glow over her figure, and diffused light over the rest of the room. She reached for a bottle of juice and drank slowly, cherishing the feeling, the solitude, imagining perhaps that Probal was somehow aware of her and was watching. He was.

The couch where he sat listening to his music was just adjacent to the kitchen and no door separated the rooms. He heard the fridge door open, saw the light and, more importantly, the figure of the woman who stood there, aroused and alone. He had moved to the entrance of the kitchen, leaning against the wall, when Mou felt his gaze. He was so still, so confident and tall.

"I'm sorry," Mou said, "did I wake you?" He laughed. Mou felt silly; of course she hadn't woken him. The music was on. He was fully dressed.

He stepped forward.

"I love Jagjit Singh," she said. He walked closer.

She looked past him at the book on the coffee table. "And Atwood." He was standing next to her now, what seemed like on top of her.

"Yes" was all he said, a yes that encouraged and playfully mocked her.

She closed the refrigerator door and leaned her back against it. He put his arm past her, hand on the fridge, creating a little wall to one side of her. He leaned in. She breathed in, closed her eyes. He kissed her.

"Come," he said, then turned and walked back to the couch he'd turned into a little bohemian haven.

She followed him, sat down. He sat next to her, slipping his hand into her nightgown, feeling for her nipples — her whole world opened up. She leaned back, let him move his body between her legs, which spread apart like lava, with no resistance. This was what she'd known of but hadn't had. This was being alive. He moved inside her again and again. They lay naked together, not thinking of Matin or of the consequences of the morning. There was only tonight. Mou opened like a flower, and Probal reveled in her beauty, her strength. He begged her for more. Begged her to stay with him, to run away with him.

She stayed a while longer, with a smile unlike one she'd ever worn. It was the smile of a woman who knew herself, who needed no one, but could enjoy life, could come alive. She dressed again and left her lover for the golden cage of her bedroom.

DUSK IN THE FROG POND

Ruby danced as she crossed one paddy bank to another. Her feet were nimble and swift and her spirits high. Her hunger pangs increased, but there was no time to eat; Munir was coming back to the village after four long months, and she had to prepare for his homecoming. The moist earth of the monsoon season was distinctively fragrant and only added to her ascending euphoria.

Munir worked in Dhaka city. He had married Ruby against his mother's wishes, but a few months after the marriage, his mother had accepted Ruby and had no further complaints. Ruby had tried her best to appeal to her mother-in-law and it had paid off.

As Ruby came home and caught hold of the brown calf to assist in milking the mother cow, her mother-in-law came out of the compound with extreme haste.

"Did you make Munir's favourite pithas?"

"Yes, Ma, I did. I am going to milk the cow now and make some milk and molasses payesh for him."

"Did you get out the fresh oil from the coconuts so my son can apply it on his hair? I heard that the city's tap water has so many chemicals that it causes hair loss."

"Yes, Ma, I did. I also ground the fresh mustard seeds to get him pure mustard oil for his dips in the pond."

"Did you take a bath yesterday?"

"No, Ma, I did not."

"I want you to take the fresh cow dung from the outer house and make a batch of fresh tablets to light the clay oven with and don't forget to put a new coat of fresh mud paste on the floor of our bedrooms and the compound."

"Yes, Ma. Then I will take a bath in the pond."

Ruby loved to dip in the pond nowadays because the lotuses were in full bloom. At this time, she forgot about the dazzling water hyacinths at the other end of the pond. She did not tell Munir that she had put a bunch of baby fishes in the pond two months ago in exchange for four bowls of rice from the storage when her mother-in-law was sleeping. The fishes must have grown by this time, and she would surprise them tomorrow by telling Munir to throw a net for lunch.

"Make sure you put on the red-and-green checkered cotton sari with the red, puffed-sleeve blouse after your bath, and don't forget to wear your silver anklets with the little bells and wear some of that jasmine essence attar."

Ruby gazed in astonishment at her mother-in-law. "Why do you want to dress me up so much?"

"Well, your husband is coming after so long. You should be a pretty and dutiful wife."

Ruby looked at her mother-law's mischievous expression. Were her eyes glinting with the hope of a grandchild? Ruby tried to think about the dates of her menstruation cycle. Her childhood friend Rini had taken so much time to explain to her the advantages of making love during a fertile period so that getting pregnant would be ten times easier. The nightly village adult education centre was teaching the housewives of her neighbourhood how to control the birth of children after having one or two.

After Ruby finished getting ready for Munir, she felt pretty excited herself as she braided her hair with the red satin ribbons that she had bought from the Poush Mela, or Poush fair. Poush, the first month of the winter season of the Bengali calendar immediately follows the harvesting season, and Ruby loved its festivities. She loved the Jatrapala, village theatre, most of all, and after watching the dance and music concerts she had bought herself matching red glass bangles with gold designs on them, as well as some muri, murki and moa for Munir. He specifically loved these snacks from the winter fair. Once she had gone with Munir to the Baul Mela and ever since she loved to hear the songs of Lalon Shah. After hearing those songs, Ruby often felt very peaceful and serene, and wondered how vastly her personal world contrasted with that of reality. She was unable to relate to the surfacing violence, hatred and jealousy in the world around her.

She'd once read about them in a book about the fairs and festivals in Bangladesh. These folk singers known as Bauls have a history spanning centuries in Bangladesh. Their nature is like that of a nomadic tribe, constantly moving from one village to another, soul-searching and believing that some higher power above them will take care of their basic needs. Survival is never a question for them, as they search their souls and fill their lives with meditation and music. Ruby often was amazed when she looked at their signature single-stringed musical instrument known as an Ektara.

Nights were difficult. As the hyenas' laughter cut the stillness of the night, her hand unconsciously went to the pillow beside her. She missed Munir beyond measure. She often whispered her innermost thoughts to the midnight blue of the night outside her wooden window where she could see the fireflies fluttering in and out of view. She needed a soulmate to speak about the trifling things of family life when everyone else was sleeping. She ached for Munir when the first kadom flowers danced in the incessant monsoon rain and when the radhachuras were ablaze with their golden glory. But she missed him most when her ovulation began and her body came alive with potential. Sometimes, the monotony of the nights would be interrupted by the wild barking of dogs or the slithering of snakes through leaves towards the rice paddies. The barking of the dogs intrigued Ruby. After a dull day of working for the harvest, it allowed her mind to fathom fascinating theories about the lives of these wild dogs; were they lonely? Were they looking for prey? Were they looking for friends? While the sinister noise of the snakes heralded no terror in Ruby's heart, her sixth sense seemed to warn her and cause a feeling of unknown dread. She would never dare to provoke them, as snakes, even in the special Jatras or plays held in her village, signalled a strange fear in her soul.

The harvest last month was very good. The huge cauldrons were all put to use as the harvested rice was boiled for hours by all the womenfolk inside and outside the house before being stored. Ruby loved the new parboiled rice, as the manual wooden dheki was operated by the neighbouring housewives, their feet in a rhythmic jump while they held on to the strong overhead ropes. This was the way the rice was separated from the husks to be cooked whenever they wanted to eat.

All the food that the women worked hard to prepare all day had to be covered and put out of reach of the stray cats. These pesky cats, who were some of Ruby's worst troubles during the day, would enter the mud and cane kitchen at will to devour her meticulously prepared food. The multicoloured jute shikkas had to be hung high up in the ceiling to hold the covered clay pots and pans with cooked foods, which were an immense temptation for these stray cats.

Setting aside those thoughts, Ruby went to the little room outside the house beside the backyard pond. A bowl of soaked rice was ready to be crushed and made into the milk payesh. She crushed a bowl of dry rice into powder with the handheld dheki. She would be making thin rice rotis for Munir with this rice flour immediately after his arrival. He loved to eat them with molasses and grated coconut. She heard the bullock cart, the bullocks crying wildly. Munir must have arrived. She finished crushing her rice, checked her braids and ran out to see.

Munir was getting down from the cart. He looked at his mother and his wife. He liked the invisible bond that he observed between them. Something intangible — he could not pinpoint it — had developed in the period that he was not there. His mother looked healthy and well-groomed. He then gazed at Ruby. What more could he want? She smelled of his favourite jasmine and looked outright gorgeous. He jumped down and started taking his bags to the house, followed by an onslaught of rain and lightning.

"So, Ma, did your chickens lay fresh eggs for me today?" asked Munir with an impish grin.

"Yes, they have given us plenty of eggs this season. I also saved up some duck eggs for you, too."

"Ruby, did you make my favourite egg curry with them?"

"Yes, with potatoes and tomatoes, and Ma has garnished them with a lot of your favourite green chili peppers and fresh coriander."

"That sounds heavenly!" said Munir as he touched his mother's feet for blessings. Ruby covered her head with the tip of her red-and-green checkered sari and touched her husband's feet. His mother put her hand on his head and blessed him. Munir caught Ruby's shoulders and brought her up from his feet where she was kneeling to touch them. He felt like crushing her to his breast and biting her lips but could not out of respect for his mother's presence. He spied the anklets on her hennaed feet and controlled his erection.

Dinner was long and tiring; Munir was exhausted from his journey. His mother repeatedly asked him questions about his rented apartment in Dhaka city, what he cooked and ate every day, did he visit her sister and his father's uncle, how his job fared, could he save any money for a rainy day, and finally, would he be staying in the village or would he go back to the city. She then applied some fresh coconut oil on his hair and started moving towards her bedroom to retire.

"Make sure you apply the oil once every week at least," she said as she made her exit. "The tap water in the city has a lot of chemicals."

"I will, Ma."

Munir waited for his mother to turn out of sight, then slid his hand inside Ruby's petticoat. With his other hand, he touched her nipples over her blouse. His parched lips touched hers as he gathered her up in his arms and moved towards their bedroom. He laid her down on the bed and gently undressed her. The flickering light of the oil lamp cast soft shadows on the contours of his wife's body and face. How he had missed her these past few months! The conversations they would have late into the night lying in each other's arms. The release of their passionate lovemaking turning to gentler tones as the nights ticked by and the dawns peeked in. He had so missed her warmth and sandalwood fragrance, which would fill his being after she returned from bathing in the pond. He could not wait anymore. As he entered her, she moaned in total abandonment. He came again and again, and she gathered every bit of his release with new vigour.

Ruby got up at dawn, and the morning sky was especially colourful and inviting. The water of the pond was a bit chilly, and the morning dew smiled upon the lotus leaves. The Moazzem was calling everyone for the morning Fajr prayers from the minaret of the village mosque. She would have to finish her bath and prayers before her mother-in-law got up or it would be very embarrassing. She looked for the two frogs who always gave her company, but she could not find them. Perhaps they also had a tiring but exhilarating night and were taking a break. They were lucky — they could sleep in, but she missed them. She got out of the pond and dried herself, then put on a generous dose of Munir's favourite talcum powder before putting on the new blue cotton sari with the golden border that he had presented to her the night before.

As she walked into the front compound of their house, the roosters were crowing. She ran to the chicken house to collect the newly laid eggs. Munir loved these eggs, still warm and fresh. She would make an omelette for him with fresh daal pooris and khola pithas made with freshly ground rice flour, eggs and salt. He liked them well done and crispy. She could not wait for lunchtime to surprise him with the fishnet and new fishes. Her mother-in-law would also have an attack of astonishment but would settle down and hug her when she saw the putees, shrimps, kechkees and beileys.

As Ruby entered the front door, she saw her mother-in-law in the kitchen fiercely blowing into the charcoals of the clay oven to get it going for breakfast. She quickly brought the end of her sari over her head to cover her wet hair. It would be extremely impolite to let her mother-in-law know that there had been passionate lovemaking last night with her son and that Ruby had to take a bath to purify herself for the morning prayers. She brought forward the newly laid chicken eggs and proudly displayed them.

"Did you know, Ma, we got two more than yesterday?"

"How marvellous! That's a great welcome for Munir. Did you not find any duck eggs?"

"I could have bet on the white and black one, she seems so ready to lay eggs, but I guess we have to wait a few more days. Or maybe the fox beat me to the duck house and took them."

"Munir loves those duck eggs sunny-side up. What a shame! Maybe tomorrow or the day after."

Munir's mother pretended that she was not seeing the drops of water falling from Ruby's wet hair and refrained from asking her if the water in the pond was cold. Ruby was a good and dutiful wife. Her parents had given her proper training. Her son had indeed made a good choice.

One evening, Ruby and her mother-in-law had been sitting in the uthan, the compound adjoining their mud-hut. It was a moonlit night and the blowing soft breeze lifted up their spirits. Besides the moonlight there was no other light around them because, after sunset, most of the kupi or oil lamps all around the other households had already been turned off. Ruby ran into the house and got a mini-radio from her bedroom and put it on the cane table between them.

"Ma, did you know that when India and Pakistan attained independence from the British, the division was mostly done based on the number of Muslims in Pakistan?"

"Ruby, I thought something to that extent. I believed that Hindus and Muslims cannot coexist in the same place, but it was not clear as I was a little girl at that time."

"Yes, Ma, even today we have the same rivalry between the Muslims in East and West Pakistan and the Hindus in India."

"But Ruby, nowadays I see that the people of East Pakistan are very proud of the Bangla language and have started hating the Urdu-speaking West Pakistanis."

"Ma, did you know that besides the language factor, unequal distribution of wealth between the two provinces, suppression of autonomy, discrimination and misappropriation of economic resources are driving a wedge between the provinces?"

"Yes, Ruby, the radio seems to be blaring the exact same topics."

"Ma, you know, I have thought about something. I really admire Sheikh Mujibur Rahman for speaking out so boldly to the West Pakistanis about nationalism and our Bengali language."

As the two women were speaking, amidst the shimmering moonlight, they never dreamt that Sheikh Mujibur Rahman would ultimately be called Bangabandhu, Father of the Nation, and would lead and inspire the Bangladeshis through the nine month long War of Independence. They never dreamt that the Bengalis of East Pakistan would sacrifice three million men, women and children for this cause. The Bangladeshis never foresaw the nine bloody months of fighting to attain independence from West Pakistan. The entire population of Bangladesh, directly or indirectly, fought for this war in any manner they could. Later, the twenty-sixth of March would be acclaimed as the Independence Day of the new nation. It was an internationally acclaimed feat, but freedom was achieved at a tremendous price. Little did Ruby and her mother-in-law know that the victory day of Bangladesh would be acknowledged on 16 December 1971. The two women were blissfully unaware of the tragedies to come, as they moved on to discussing their excitement about Munir's upcoming visit from the city.

Munir entered the kitchen freshly bathed and wearing a cotton *genji* and a striped cotton lungi. He loved the commotion his wife and mother were making to prepare his breakfast. He thought of his solitary life in the city, mutely making and eating his meagre meals: breakfast, which consisted of two slices of bread with butter and jam and a cup of strong tea, a quick lunch of rice and meat or vegetables, then a lonely, cold supper. This would all come to an end if he could convince his mother and move her along with Ruby to the city. He knew it would be a hard battle, but signs of political turmoil were brewing up all across the country, especially in the urban areas. His mother would not want to leave the house and land that she had come to as a young bride so many years ago. She had so many memories of his father in this house, of Munir growing up, of close relatives coming and spending good times. She wanted to breathe her last breath on her husband's property. She seemed to think that Munir did not understand this.

Munir and Ruby went to the village panchayeth that evening. A meeting of the village elders was taking place to give the verdict and punishment for an adulterer, as well as two teenagers who had been charged with rounding up children as young as twelve to take part in planting car bombs during hartals, or strikes, and curfews called by the opposition party. The political situation was getting so tense that all people, young and old, were beginning to be involved in this fight for liberation. Munir was glad that he had agreed and made the effort to attend. The married woman was cleared of all accusations after many witnesses testified about the soundness of her character and the complainant turned out to be a leech who had been turned down by the woman when he had requested sexual favours. The two boys were found guilty, and lenient punishment was doled out to them in the form of community and voluntary work, considering their tender ages. They were also ordered to go back to their high school studies and not to disturb any underage children for violent work. It was quite late when everything was over. The village headman thanked them for coming and saw them off in a rickshaw home.

There was a full moon, and a sweet Falguni breeze; the caress of this sweet breeze was gentle on Ruby's skin and only came by in Falgun, the eleventh month of the Bengali calendar. They sat in the beautifully painted rickshaw as Munir's mind escalated higher; he felt happy and his entire being was overflowing with unknown elation. He gently took Ruby's hand in his own and whistled a tune. The rickshaw puller looked back and laughed out loud.

"I recognize that tune. The folk queen Momtaz sang it in the village mela."

"Yes!"

"Faitta jai... Faitta jai... my heart is bursting because you are walking hand in hand with another girl while passing my front courtyard... "

"Did you know that Momtaz has earned a spot in the *Guinness Book of Records* for the most songs recorded in a single day?"

"Is that so? I am so impressed! Makes me feel proud to be a Bangladeshi!"

Munir went on whistling another popular romantic melody: "Ei raat tomar a amar... Ei khon tomar a amar... This night is yours and mine... This moment is ours... "

Ruby clutched Munir's hand a bit tighter. She gazed up at the sky with its countless twinkling stars and felt life was exquisite. She must add some extra prayers to her Esha prayers tonight to thank Allah the Almighty for giving her such endless happiness. Munir asked the rickshaw man to stop at a paan or betel leaf corner store. He bought two sweet Moheshkhali paan stuffed with every imaginable kind of paan masala and popped one into Ruby's mouth.

"So that I can taste the sweetness of your mouth tonight" — Moheshkhali and Chittagong produced the sweetest paan leaves in Bangladesh. Ruby blushed as Munir intently watched the bright red colour of the paan, choon, zarda and khoyer slowly seep into her full, pouting lips.

Then came the blackest night of their lives — the twenty-sixth of March 1971. The Bangladesh Liberation War. The authorities of West Pakistan did not want to hand over the country's power to the people of East Pakistan, although they had an elected majority. It was during this war that Munir suffered one of the biggest losses of his life. As he participated in the War of Freedom, he continuously learned new things. He recorded, added and discarded information every minute as his mind raced against time. The Razakars, Al-Badars and Al-Shams were local groupings of the Pakistani Army, and they were abetting and helping the West Pakistani soldiers in their crimes. They had turned their backs on their birthplace and became traitors to their own motherland. They raped, looted and vandalized relentlessly, along with the West Pakistani soldiers. The ticking clock in his brain recorded his feeling of nausea and condemnation of these local groupings working with the West Pakistani army, and he was aghast at the anti-forces of his beloved East Pakistan. Munir was absolutely shocked as they victimized the Hindus and minorities in East Pakistan. Hindus were checked for circumcision, and other religious minorities were asked to recite verses from the Holy Quran.

Then one dark night, a group of West Pakistani soldiers entered Munir and Ruby's home. Munir was participating in an operation with the Freedom Fighters where they were trying to blow up the only bridge taking traffic from the city to the village so that those animals could not bring additional war supplies to the village to facilitate internal aggression.

He was second-in-command to this Freedom Fighters Battalion and his chief had just lost one of his legs in the previous night's operation, so Munir had to leave his mother and Ruby alone that night. While he poured himself into the task at hand, he had a strange premonition and couldn't shake the fear that everything would not be all right when he returned home. Along with that fear, he felt that ticking time bomb in his mind, his sixth sense repeatedly warning him that he was running out of time. But for what? Or for whom?

It was almost dawn when he returned home. They had been successful with the bridge but there was a lot of pain in Munir's right hand. He had not eaten since morning and craved water-dipped rice, or panta bhaat, with green chili peppers. Ruby would be waiting for him with that and a kerosine lamp. As he passed the pond outside his house, he heard the frogs croaking in unison. Why were they up? And why were they croaking so loudly when there was not the slightest trace of rainfall?

The kitchen door was open in the outer house. How come Ruby forgot to close it? She usually checked it a few times before going to bed. There were a few cats fighting for the leftover food from the night before. Their growling was violent, and as he passed his mother's room, he was surprised to find her door half open. He entered the room. Sometimes, his mother forgot to pull down the mosquito net and mosquitoes would swarm all over her. Malaria was rampant and he did not want her to suffer. As he crossed the threshold, he felt something wet seeping through his flip-flops. He flicked his cigarette lighter and directed the light towards the floor. Was it blood? His heart missed a beat. Then he saw his mother's hookah turned upside-down on the ground. There were charcoals and tobacco all over the floor. His mother loved to smoke from the pipe of the hookah, or sheesh, before going to bed. The gurgling sound of the water in the brass bottom had often put him to sleep when he was a teenager. As he turned his lighter towards his mother's bed, he saw her lifeless body. He quickly brought out the flashlight from under his mother's pillow and turned it on her body. She had no clothes on. Her breasts and lips had been sliced off. Her white hair had been pulled out of her head. Strands lay in a pile beside her pillow. Her eyes had been scraped out. He mechanically covered her body with the old cane mat hanging on the wall, which she had used for offering her prayers five times a day. He sat down on the cold mud floor beside his mother's feet. He put his head on her feet and sobbed uncontrollably for a few minutes. All at once, he felt blood on his cheeks. The blood was oozing from her toenails, which had been pulled out. His heart shattered into pieces and he sat there with a stoic look on his face; he felt infinitely dazed. He then wiped his face with his sleeve and got up.

He slowly walked towards his own bedroom. The door was also open, and as dawn was breaking, there were a little light coming in from the window of his bedroom. At first he thought Ruby was also dead. She was not moving at all. He ran to the kitchen and brought a glass of water from the terracotta kolshi. He sprinkled it on her face, and her eyelids flickered. He sprinkled some more cold water on her eyes, cheeks and neck. Gradually her cold body became warm, but she would not open her eyes. Her blouse was ripped in places and she only had her petticoat on. There were bite marks all over her cheeks, neck, hips and breasts. She kept her eyes closed as she coldly said, "I am going to jump into the frog pond now and never come back."

"How can I survive without Mother or you?" asked a dazed Munir.

"What happened to Mother?" Ruby murmured, then slipped out of consciousness.

Munir went to the iron chest where Ruby kept all her favourite belongings. He took out her red-and-gold Banarasi silk sari, which he had given her for her wedding, the red satin petticoat and the matching red-and-gold blouse. He washed her body and all her bite marks and bruises with hot water and applied an antiseptic balm. Then he dressed her in the petticoat and blouse and finally the sari. He combed her hair into a braid and applied powder, lipstick and kajal. As he was spraying perfume on her, she opened her eyes.

"Have you become mad, Munir?" she whispered with all the strength she possessed. She gazed at her sari incredulously.

"No, but I will, if you speak another word."

He then called the Quazi of the village, who came and solemnized their wedding once again.

He began the funeral preparations for his mother.

Five years later, Munir, Ruby and Lily sat by the frog pond in the crimson aura of the setting sun. Lily was holding a jar of caterpillars and trying to caress the little leaves of the lojjaboti, the touch-me-not plant, which instantly closed upon human touch. Ruby gazed at Munir with infinite respect and love. If it was not for him, she would not be living today. He had held her hand through thick and thin. He had forbidden her from ending her life. He had not revealed to anyone the details of that horrifying night. He had accepted Lily as his own daughter after she was born the next year. Allah did not give them any more children, but Lily filled their lives. She jumped into the frog pond, collecting caterpillars and tadpoles, in spite of her mother forbidding her to do so countless times. The little girl mischievously gazed at her father and softly asked, "Baba, do you want to race me to the other end?"

"I will, if you let those caterpillars go," smiled Munir.

"But Baba, these are my pets and I love to watch them eat!"

"If you let them out, they will turn to beautiful butterflies and fill the world with their colours."

"There are so many other colours in this world, why do we need more?" pouted Lily.

"You naughty girl, you will catch a cold from the pond water, especially in this chilly weather," said Ruby as she wrapped a woolen shawl over Munir's shoulders. Then she pointed to Lily and held out a sweater for her.

"Well, let's see." She got hold of a frog before it could jump away, kissed it and threw it back on a big kachuripana leaf. "There are the colours of the rainbow, the colours of the flowers and fruits, the colours of the sun, moon and stars," went on a grave Lily.

"But everything has its own colour, yet we need other colours to compliment them," said Munir.

"Yes, Baba like I have my own colour, yet I need a brother or a sister to compliment me. You agree with me, Baba?"

"Yes, angel, pray to Allah and He might grant your wish," Ruby said softly.

Dusk was descending on the frog pond. Crickets sang and the fireflies were starting their glowing journey. Munir spotted a water snake at the far end of the pond and slipped into the water between his daughter and the creature. He could not keep her from harm, but he could be there, ready, if and when it came.

MONSOON BREEZE

It is rare that we get what we set out for, finding ourselves more often than not in the situation we'd tried so hard to avoid. To our surprise, we find we've inadvertently wandered into the life others had sought. We find ourselves the recipients of their envy for the very thing we regret.

Brishti had met Bob ten years ago. It was a cold afternoon in mid-January. Snow formed small walls on either side of the sidewalks as she walked briskly in her old pair of leather boots. The virgin white snow seemed to quiver in expectation. It would be only a few hours before the slush and traffic would turn the whiteness to a dark hue of grey and black.

The night before had been particularly violent. Her husband Alam had been planning to return to Bangladesh again, a trip for which Brishti had to pay and for which she felt she suffered. She asked him to stay, to get a job, to apply himself to this new country the way she had. It was her birthday. Everything felt like a betrayal, and she was not able, as she usually was, to hold it all in.

"I thought I'd come home from work to yellow roses, a nice dinner; instead you're halfway through that bottle and making plans to leave again."

That was when he hit her, again. It was at times like this that her mind escaped her body and nestled with the rainfall of the Aashaarh month in Bangladesh, which showed no signs of letting up. Just like Alam. Many times in the past, she had tightened a shawl around her shoulders and sped towards the riverbank, hoping to miss the worst of it, just like her husband's mood swings. This was her repeated imaginative escape from Alam's violence and abuse. She would be only paces away from her parents' front door, which was gradually looming up, when a monsoon breeze would sweep through the street and nearly knock her over. It would be electric; she would feel she had sprouted wings and went flying with increasing speed through layers of dazzling cloud and directly into Bob's warm embrace.

Brishti shivered as the cold swept through her clothes, intermittently like a tidal wave. It was one of those grey-to-the-bone days, had been like that for weeks. There was so much she'd wanted to do, and it seemed now that there was so little time in which to do it. It had been an especially hard day for her. Her feelings of humiliation and abasement from last night stung her more sharply than both Alam's hands and the harsh cutting winds of the brutal Toronto winter. However, it was on this day that Brishti met Bob for the first time at a Second Cup at the end of her street. It was something about his eyes, the warmth in them, the attentiveness, that caught her attention, that held it.

He came to her table, leaned in, unaggressive but confident. "Would you mind if I asked you out to dinner tomorrow evening?"

He hadn't asked her name, hadn't seemed to flinch at the ring on her finger. There was something so presumptuous about it and yet so inviting. She admired his boldness, and it seemed both of them already knew she would say yes.

They met the following day in an adjacent neighbourhood, at eight p.m., for sushi.

He arrived with yellow roses, and she took it as a sign. He held her gaze, touched her hand, dressed well, spoke well, made her want him almost against her will.

He hugged her at the end of the meal, a tight, genuine embrace, and on the way home she sang quietly to herself, "Kothar toh shesh nei, mon chai bole jai… Amar moner kotha olpo noy…" — *There is no end to words, I feel like going on and on… My heart has so much to say…*

Alam stood by the door when she arrived. "Where have you been?" He'd been waiting. He was drunk.

"I had to work late."

"Dressed up like that? With full makeup? Come on!" He took her arm. "You think I am a fool?"

Brishti jerked her arm away from him. He slapped her cheek. She did not flinch. His violence had lost its effect, so common was it by now.

She noticed empty packets of parathas and chicken curry, beer cans. Immigrating to Canada had only made things worse. He was a medical practitioner in Bangladesh but had failed all his equivalency tests in Canada. He could have driven a cab or worked as a busboy but said that was below him.

The next morning, as Brishti readied herself for work, she listened to an interview on the CBC. A businessman answered the question, "What is your idea of happiness?" He had replied in a contemptible manner about how his rare gem collection, his sports cars and his private jet were enough to keep him happy.

How obnoxious! Well, keep on dreaming buddy, Brishti thought.

Bob never spoke about his ex-wife, and Brishti never mentioned Alam. The winters had turned to springs and summers, and they felt there was never enough time. They had talked often about running away together to Bangladesh, and now it was finally happening. Bob loved the idea, and Brishti was intent on making it happen.

They had worked it out in detail. Brishti was to withdraw her funds and leave a letter for Alam before leaving to meet Bob at the airport.

It all became more real as she placed not only the letter but the divorce papers she'd had drawn up on Alam's pillow. She could not tell what she was feeling. Excitement had quieted her doubts and fears. Everything else was a fog. Life with Bob in Bangladesh would be different but not hard. She would miss a lot about Canada, of course: the freedom of movement, the choice of eating whatever you want at any time, the values of free speech. She loved the purity of the snow in winter and the dazzling bounty of her favourite fruits and vegetables in the summer. She was still amazed at the autumn glory during fall and the sheer relaxation and enjoyment in people's hearts during Saturdays and Sundays. She had looked in awe when fortunate people helped others in less fortunate situations without any personal gains. The respect and love displayed to the elders, the handicapped and the helpless ones. And of course she would miss this all, but now she had love. She had someone who valued her and a chance to be alone and happy with him. She had to take it.

She couldn't wait to introduce Bob to the world she had left behind, that she considered, to this day, to be her true home. There was warmth there, a celebration of authenticity, a pleasure in the small, the natural, and above all, there was the indomitable resilience of Bangladesh, which was the source of her own strength.

Bob came running to her with the excitement of a boy one spring morning before they'd made their move. "Do you think I will like the krishnachura blossoms? Or the radhachuras? Or the bougainvillea climbing up like vine roses?"

"Wait a minute, who told you about these?"

"I was visiting Thailand and the tourist guide pointed out these flowers there and compared them to those in India, Pakistan and Bangladesh."

"You can also see kathal chapa and rojonigandha, like the ones you saw in Malaysia."

Bob's eyes were dreamy as he made love to her that evening, and Brishti felt he was already in Bangladesh. She had to tell him minute details about many tourist spots, about Cox's Bazar, the longest uncultivated beach in the world, the mangrove forest of Sundarban in Khulna where the famous Royal Bengal tigers still prowled, Ahsan Manzil Museum, Pari Bibi's tomb, Rangamati and Kaptai.

As Brishti and Bob got out of the airplane in Bangladesh, the twilight sky was in a glorious splendour. They had gone with the Quazi to the downtown mosque located at Dundas and Chestnut the night before to have their Nikkah done to legalize their marriage.

Their union felt different and complete. It must have rained the night before. The damp musk fragrance coming from the earth lifted her mood. She always shared a special connection to this monsoon rain. Flashbacks set in as Brishti thought about how she used scenarios of her favourite rainy days as a method to escape into her illusive world of imagination during her marriage with Alam. No wonder the meaning of her name, Brishti, is rain! Nostalgia set in. There was no place in this world like Dhaka. Brishti felt like bowing her head to her beloved motherland.

She held Bob's hand and waved at everyone. She saw the beloved faces of her father and mother. Her younger brother Hira and younger sister Moni had also come. The blast of hot humid air hit them strongly. Moni gazed at Bob with a trace of hesitation.

"Can you speak Bangla?"

"Just try me!" smiled Bob.

"But you are white, and I will not understand your accent," exclaimed Moni.

"Then you can learn English and talk to me properly," reasoned Bob.

"But you have come to Bangladesh, and you are the one who should learn, not me."

"If you want to go to Canada then you must learn English, no way out," reprimanded Bob.

"But you married my sister and it is your obligation to speak in Bangla," butted in Hira.

"Okay, okay, but you guys have to teach me, that is my condition."

Brishti bent down and touched her parents' feet for blessings. Bob followed suit, and Hira and Moni squealed in delight. This was going to be absolutely hilarious.

Bob heartily enjoyed the exotic Bangladeshi food that evening. The fresh gourd fried with thinly sliced potatoes, the homegrown tomatoes baked and squashed into a bhorta with hot green chili peppers, sliced onions, fresh chopped coriander and mustard oil with steamed fragrant jasmine rice was heavenly. The shutki or dried shrimp cooked with eggplant into a curry was a bit too spicy but tasted scrumptious. And at dawn when he saw the drooping white and orange shefalis on the moist grass in the backyard, it took Brishti quite a long time to explain to him this miracle of nature. Why the shefalis could not face the sunrise and fell on the grass. Bob was wearing a lungi, a sarong-like garment that is wrapped around the waist and tied with a knot. It was presented to him by Hira but was so tricky and difficult that he was already having second thoughts about wearing it again. Though he had to admit, it was so easy doing certain things while wearing it.

The next morning, breakfast was sent over for the new groom and bride by relatives and friends: Haji's biryani from Old Dhaka, Shorshe Ilish the national fish of Bangladesh cooked with mustard seed paste, pithas which were various handmade sweet cakes made with rice flour, and freshly made yogurt directly from the dairy farm. Bob was amazed, and Brishti and her siblings lost their breath laughing at his experimentation with various local Bangladeshi cuisine. Mango, jackfruit, lychee and other tropical fruits were sent by others in baskets. He learned a few of the names of the local mangoes, so different from the ones that were found in Canada: Foria, Bombai, Kohitoor, Laksmanbhog, Khisraphat, Ashhwina, Khisanbhog, Kuapahadi, Laya, Mohanbhog and Misribhog. Then the Quazi or religious priest was brought over to once again convert Bob into a Muslim, so that Brishti's family could be a part of this beautiful transition.

Brishti's mom was lighting a bonfire in their front yard. She was happy but apprehensive. She took out a tiny brass container and held it over the smoke of that fire. She softly recited Surah Yaseen from the Holy Quran. Brishti had frequently called her mother sobbing in frustration and pain. It had broken her heart to hear about the physical and emotional burden her daughter had to bear every minute she was with Alam, suffering from his ruthlessness. Brishti had many a time begged her parents for their permission to get out of that marriage. The fire burned brightly as layers of soot became heavy on the container. She would take an applicator tomorrow and apply a tiny round spot of this black kajal behind Bob's ear. This would protect him from all evil eyes. Bob might not be from their culture, he might not have known the Bengali language, but he was a good person. Her heart was saying that. Above all, he was a human being and his blood was also red like theirs.

And this time, Brishti deserved to be happy.

SHADOW OVER THE HENNA TREE

Helen had no fight left. She sat on the stairs by the hallway, wondering about the state of her heart, trying to remember if she'd taken her medication that morning or the morning before. It was midnight when Angela walked in the door, red-eyed and wired. Now she stood there in her evening clothes, raging. Angela was Helen's youngest daughter, and her most difficult. This was their third argument of the week. It was always something: a low grade, missed curfew, a moment of disrespect. Helen didn't want to fight, but she felt this need for her daughter to understand, to have compassion for the way her increasing disregard was affecting her mother. A few weeks prior, Helen had visited the doctor to inquire about antidepressants. She'd been losing energy, feeling hopeless, depleted. She couldn't help but blame her daughter to some degree, and so with each transgression her spite grew.

Angela was standing in the hallway like a boxer ready to pounce. "Dad's absence doesn't make me your keeper, Mom."

"I'm not looking for you to be my keeper. I'm looking for you to keep yourself safe."

"I am safe."

"And how do I know that when you're out so late?"

"That's your problem, Mom. Not mine. You want me to be like all your friends' little perfect Pakistani and Bengali daughters, like the girls who stay home all day sweeping and doing their homework, who barely have friends. Well, too bad. I'm not like them. I'm like Canadian girls and I like it that way. It's not the end of the world."

"My heart hurts. My diabetes is acting up again. Why do you need to aggravate my condition?"

"Why do you have to care so much? This world is not only about you!"

Angela stumbled past her mother, up the stairs, and in typical teenage form, slammed her door.

More often than not these days, Helen regretted having made the move to Canada. Bangladesh, with its warmth and tradition, its expansiveness, was more a part of her than any aspect of this new country. She had followed her husband here when Angela was three. He'd come just before her birth for work and gave word for the family to follow once he felt secure enough in his endeavours. Helen remembered the first spring of her arrival. The tulips were in full bloom, and everything seemed lush, full of potential. For the first few years she relished the seasons, the stark white gleaming snow, the striking colours of autumn, the birds, the squirrels, the wide empty streets and the sense of quiet, of safety. She thanked the Almighty Creator for this new opportunity, but over the years her zeal had worn thin.

Angela was the only one of her children who considered herself more Canadian than Bangladeshi. With every passing year her memories of the place in which she was born blurred and dissipated. She was raised on Dr. Spock's philosophies, wore mass-produced diapers, then sports bras and Fruit of the Loom panties.

Helen thought of her own mother back home in Bangladesh, making do with small handmade stitched kathas and rubber cloths on the bed and rubber panties. On sunny afternoons, the clotheslines would be a rainbow of kathas and reusable cotton diapers. This was a part of every week growing up for her and her five siblings, every week save for the monsoon seasons, when Baishakhi storms made any outdoor activity impossible. She often used the memory of her mother, of her tireless washing and rewashing of garments, as a stabilizing force. Thinking of those days in Bangladesh brought great calm. All seemed right. All seemed manageable.

Everything was different here. While Helen had grown up slowly, with timid hesitation, Angela was a force. By fifteen, she seemed intent on taking over the world. She spoke boldly and shared her opinions, which were many, with anyone who would listen. One day, when Helen had worked a particularly late shift, she came home to find Angela unconscious on the doorstep, one hand in her purse, one on the ground, under her head. She had overdosed and needed to have her stomach pumped. As Helen sat in the hospital, holding her daughter's hand, she reprimanded herself, searching deeply for what she had done wrong. She wanted to call her husband, but he was in Hong Kong on business. The call would go as it always had. He would tell her he was busy, that she should be equipped to handle this on her own, that it was her job to do so. To call him would be viewed a failure. Helen was intent, in this situation more than any, to succeed.

Angela had slumped over the couch like an animated corpse the following day. Her stomach had been emptied. She drank tea slowly, agonizingly, pleaded with her mother.

"This will never happen again." She was so pale.

"Please believe me. Please understand things are different in Canada. It's so hard," she said. "I will pray five times a day. I will learn Bengali. I will be the perfect daughter again. I'm so sorry, Mother."

Helen slouched in a deep chair next to her daughter, a faraway expression of worry on her face, a slow shutting down of emotion. She was beginning to feel numb.

"Okay, dear. We will see" was all she could bring herself to say. There was no more fight, no more expectation. It just was what it was.

Weeks passed, then months, without incident. At the end of the school year, Angela found out she had made the honour roll.

She was at the top of her class in most subjects. As she sat in the audience watching her daughter receive her certificates, Helen couldn't help but feel dejected. It gave Angela a false sense of accomplishment. There was her daughter, feeling as though all was repaired in light of good grades. But good grades weren't the point for Helen; respect was, good health, some semblance of the homeland. Nothing Angela could do would bring her ease, and the more Angela sulked, the more aware Helen became that she was incapable of being satisfied when it came to her daughter.

Angela laughed with her friends, looked proudly over her accolades and didn't notice for a second the distress her mother was in.

When Angela's father, Probal, returned from abroad, the mood shifted even further downwards. He had failed to secure whatever contract he'd been working on. Helen had no time to understand her husband's work. It was abstract, far away, seemingly impossible to grasp. She watched him come and go, celebrate and mourn, all with a supportive wife's loving detachment. His presence now added pressure, and the failure of his contract made approaching him about Angela that much more delicate a task. He didn't need more stress, didn't need to know that Helen was incapable of holding down the fort in his absence. She knew all of this and respected it, but so often she wished for his partnership, his presence, his guidance. She'd been thinking of sending Angela to private school but was afraid that proposing it would only aggravate Probal's sense of having failed financially. And so she was caught like this between her daughter and her husband, forever unable to do right by them entirely, ever unable to be entirely happy herself.

Probal stayed a few weeks, then packed and departed again, this time for Chicago. Angela began a new school year, still intent on keeping her word to her mother. Things seemed okay for a while. Helen even found herself enjoying prolonged afternoons with her friends, without much to complain about. She was able to listen, to be present; she hadn't taken her antidepressants and saw, at this point, no need for them.

Midway through the year Helen approached the parent-teacher meeting with airy optimism, excited to discuss her daughter's good grades. The school was a short walk from home, and though it was mid-winter, it was mild out, windless. Helen arrived, unwrapped a scarf from her head and took a seat across from Angela's homeroom teacher. There were the usual niceties, the offering of a glass of water, comments about the weather. Then, more suddenly than Helen was prepared for, the teacher's face went stern; a little frown appeared. All optimism drained from Helen's being in that single moment, that terrible shift.

"Angela is not a bad student," the teacher said, "but she is struggling."

"With what?" Helen knew her daughter to be impeccably sharp, more intelligent than most adults she knew.

"Not academically. Angela is a very good student. The trouble is with her behaviour. She breaks rules, almost as a point; not big rules mind you, little things like not turning in her student card at the front desk. It's not a huge transgression, of course, but it shows intentional rebellion, sets her apart from the others. Sets a bad example. Let me ask you something, is Angela's father around much?"

Helen froze. She didn't want to answer the question. She wanted to stand up and leave, forget this conversation ever happened. She felt hopeless, infantilized.

"He travels for work."

"I see."

"Do you suspect that has any correlation with Angela's issues?"

"I believe Angela is acting out of a desire for attention, her father's attention."

"I see."

Helen noticed her hand shaking as she lifted her glass of water to her mouth. She put it down and excused herself. There was no way she could stay after this, nothing more she could say. That night she cried into her pillow. So much of this life was beyond her control, so much was not right. She thought of her friends who had immigrated, how many of them struggled with similar issues, how many worried about the mental state of their children in the West. Mental illness was on the rise in Canada, as was drug use and sexual activity among teens. There were resources in place here, of course, language and education centres, guidance counsellors, education and employment opportunities, qualification and equivalency exams, subsidized housing. Even with all of this, the strain of uprooting, of adjusting to a new climate, a new way of being, was too much for most, and many broke under the strain. Helen didn't want to fall victim to this. She fought it, tried to stay positive, but hearing that Angela was suffering, for want of her father, hit her harder than she could have imagined. It hit her, perhaps, because she suffered without Probal too. She wanted more than financial security. She wanted companionship, a masculine presence, someone to share with, to be consoled by. She wanted Probal, and clearly her daughter did as well.

That night, when Angela came home late from a study group up the street, Helen felt a new camaraderie. Instead of being upset, she made herself and Angela tea, sat with her and asked, with total sincerity, how her daughter was feeling. It was as though Angela had been waiting for this all along. She eased into her seat, held the warm mug in her hands and began to talk. She told her mother about her friends, about one girl who'd found out she was pregnant, just one year older than she was. The girl's name was Sheuli, another Bengali girl. She said the girl was at odds with her mother, who wanted her to get an abortion. She said there'd been an altercation, something about Sheuli being hit with a rolling pin, something about calling the police. Angela had hours' worth of stories like this. Helen listened, nodding, absorbing the full breadth of it all. Angela paused after a while and smiled.

"I wasn't sure when the best time to tell you this was," she said. "I feel like it's now."

Helen clutched her heart, imagining the worst. "Go on," she said with calm but poignant fear.

"I've been accepted to McGill in Montreal, a full scholarship. It's my dream school, Mom. Are you happy for me?"

Helen was overcome with a rare sort of calm. She saw in her daughter a Canadian girl with academic aspirations and a sense of self, of ambition. She saw that this was okay. She saw what they were both up against, the chaos of life in this country, the adjustments one had to make in one's thinking, and had, for the first time since moving to Canada, a sense of her and her daughter's strength. She felt confident. She trusted Angela, saw in her a girl who was caught between two worlds and who was trying her best. She saw in her the possibility of a future, a future better than any she could have imagined before this moment.

"I am happy for you," she said. And she meant it.

THE DOOR
REMAINS CLOSED

Aftab Bhai, the marriage-maker, wanted ten thousand taka for having provided the family with a suitable bride. Five thousand, if the prospective groom and his parents liked the details of the girl, and five thousand upon completion of the first meeting between the future bride and groom. He sat with the groom's father, counting out the first installment. It was short, just three thousand. Aftab stopped chewing and spurted red betel leaf juice over his silk kurti.

"I am supposed to receive five thousand, not three!" His fingers were dirty, nails broken and unkempt. He snatched the bride's bio-data and passport photo back with indignation.

Modhu's father was taken aback. He squinted at Aftab Bhai. "I like the bio-data. I think I might have counted the money wrong."

"There are many grooms for this girl. Amongst my one hundred applications this is one of the best." He washed the betel juice from his kurti and popped a fresh paan into his mouth, with betel nut cut ever so thinly by his wife and mixed with paan Bahar and zarda. This paan leaf was special, the sweet variety grown only in Chittagong.

"Did I not say I had made a mistake?" growled Modhu's father. He understood that he could not swindle Aftab Bhai in any manner. Moreover, Modhu was becoming more difficult by the day. He had reports from two sources that people had spotted him going into the red-light districts. Why blame the boy? He also had to release himself from his physical urges when he was Modhu's age. This girl looked pretty, though her family was not ideal. Time was running out. He grudgingly brought out two thousand taka, which he had hidden in the secret pocket of his underwear.

"Do I have to count again?" Aftab Bhai asked.

"Make sure you do not show this girl's bio to anyone else."

Aftab Bhai grabbed the money and gave Modhu's parents back the picture and bio. He had a gnawing certainty that his matchmaking would strike gold in this case.

Next week, Modhu and his parents went to see Maya. Her parents were not as bad as Modhu's father had imagined. They were lower middle class but talked with softness and dignity. Maya was dressed up in a pink-and-gold sari, wore barely any makeup. As she entered the room, holding a tray with small sherbet glasses of Rooh Afza, the room lit up. She had this inherent beauty and quiet determination as she softly tread across the mosaic floor. Modhu and his parents checked her walking, asked her a few questions about her studies and qualifications, checked her tone and pronunciation of words, checked how long her tresses were and asked whether she had any objections to living with Modhu's family. Her accent did not reflect the tone of her parents' distinctive regional dialect. She fixed her eyes on the floor when speaking to elders and was suitably quiet.

Maya's father requested a modest Mehr, the obligatory monetary promise that is given to the bride in a Muslim wedding. This was happily accepted, and a wedding date was set.

Maya glowed on the day of her wedding. Her sisters and cousins bathed her. They rubbed yellow paste comprising freshly ground turmeric, shondhi, sandalwood and twenty-five other spices mixed with fresh milk over her body to make her skin soft, fragrant and sparklingly bright. Her friends and neighbours sang wedding songs loudly in off-key celebration. Rice cakes and pithas were freshly made on a clay oven in the courtyard and distributed amongst the guests who wore yellow- and red-coloured saris with roses. Marigolds adorned their hair.

After the ritual bath, ornate henna was applied to her palms and feet. The blackish-red patterns were then sprinkled with gold and silver sparkles. Her cousins teased her about the dark red colour, which had seeped into her skin.

"The darker the henna colour, the more your husband will love you, Maya Apu," said Sophia, her sixteen-year-old cousin. She had come all the way from America to attend the wedding.

"Where did you hear that?" Maya was thrown off.

"I once heard Madonna say that while applying henna design on her body for a song release."

"I do not know how much I will be loved, but I do know he is the first and last man in my life."

"Maya Apu, why should he be the last man? You never know with these old-fashioned arranged marriages whether you can settle with him for life or not."

"This marriage is in my destiny and whether I will be happy or not is also written in the stars," said Maya softly.

Modhu and Maya were very happy. They taught at a secondary school and seemed to have fluid, complimentary demeanours. In the developing world, the middle class is sandwiched between the lower and upper. In this position, pride is everything. Maya had once read that during periods of famine and natural disasters, it was only the very needy who lined up to receive food and other relief. The middle class, in spite of their pangs of hunger, found it below their dignity and pride, which stopped them from lining up. The middle class have enough money to get by, but never much left. They are like imprisoned birds, allowed to flap their wings but not to fly.

Within five years, the couple had two children, Salman and Seema. They were happy together, enjoying the fruits of the life they were building. But their happiness did not endure. Modhu was transferred to Dhaka to teach. He had only thirty days to get ready and move. As Maya rested her head on her beloved's shoulder the night before he left, she felt the cramps of a sadness. They would be separated for the first time in their married life.

"I know your days will pass very slowly without the children and me, but you will be home for the Eid holidays, right?" Her tears were ceaseless.

"Don't be silly. Of course, I will be home for the two Eids," said Modhu, wiping Maya's tears.

"How can you eat the food cooked by a maid when you have always eaten food that I have cooked?" Maya looked at the sky with the fluffy white clouds, yearning to have their mobility, to up and drift to wherever Modhu was.

"I will think about you as I eat, and when I come home I will eat you!" teased Modhu as he tenderly slipped his hand down her blouse, felt her nipples harden. He had no idea how he was going to cope with not having her beside him every night.

She smelled his musky scent and felt his hardness and became moist. It was the most fulfilling night they'd spent together.

Life moved on. Maya counted the droplets of the monsoon rain falling on her window with unbearable pathos as she passed sleepless nights yearning for her husband. The rainy season slowly turned to summer, Hemanta, then winter and spring, and it was time for Modhu's homecoming holiday. Maya applied joba kusum lakhhi bilash, fragrant oil, to her black tresses. She scrubbed her body with turmeric powder and milk because Modhu liked the smell, then coloured her nails and hands with fresh henna paste. She bought new clothes for Salman and Seema because both had grown since the last time their father had seen them. The day that he was supposed to come, she put on his favourite red cotton sari with a thick gold border. She applied kajal to both her eyes and put a matching red bindi on her forehead. She chewed betel leaves with choon and zarda so that her lips would be crimson and her breath would be sweet.

Maya finished at school and quickly came home. She made a big glass of lemonade and put it away. She would serve it with lots of crushed ice when Modhu arrived. She cooked his favourite curry of Pabda fish and Ilish fish with tamarind. She had put aside the prawns with shells for the next day. Salman and Seema had finished their homework and were counting the minutes.

She was taken aback when her father-in-law entered the room with an agitated air. "We just got news that Modhu is not coming," he said.

"But dada, he promised us!" said Salman and Seema.

"He fell sick and he cannot make the journey," said Modhu's dad in a low, cold voice.

The children were crying, and both Maya and their grandfather could not find words to console them. After they left the room, he told Maya the truth.

Modhu had remarried last week. Islam allows a man to have up to four wives, provided the first wife gives him permission to take a second wife. Modhu received no such permission and was liable to being sued by Maya if she wanted, but he still took such a great risk. In a brief note to his father, he wrote that he had acted out of the necessity of his isolation. He had married a colleague who was also distanced from her family. They'd found solace in one another. He assured his father that he would always take care of Maya and the children, that they were his first responsibility. He hoped for forgiveness.

In a fury, Maya threw her wedding ornaments in the trash and thought no more of them. She focused all her mental, physical and economic resources into bringing Salman and Seema up in this world of uncertainty. She ingrained in her children the necessity of preparing for the worst.

Modhu tried to come back a few times to meet Maya and his son and daughter. They didn't allow it even once, and eventually he gave up. Maya believed that eventually Modhu settled his mind and heart towards his new family. She had heard about his new family, children and life in Dhaka. Often there were factors in a person's life that were beyond one's control. You can just attribute it to destiny. You cannot rationalize it, however much you try. Life moves on no matter what; so did Maya.

She lost count of the cycles of summers and winters that elapsed at a steady pace. Once again, the monsoon season was sweeping over the city. Salman had become a successful doctor and Seema, a bright electrical engineer. While their professional lives flourished, they struggled with relationships, unable to commit. The previous summer they had gone to visit their cousin in Toronto who sent them return tickets as graduation presents. They loved the beautiful structure of the CN Tower and the quaint shops at Kensington market.

They went to the Little Bangladesh of North America, a neighbourhood of Bengalis in Toronto. There were familiar sign boards and grocery stores, as well social assistance institutions for seniors and new immigrants. The schools had Bangladeshi settlement councillors who assisted parents and students to acclimatize to their new homes.

They were touched to have found a tiny part of their motherland and helping hands in unknown territory. It was the highlight of their trip.

They wished their mom had accompanied them to see all this. Salman bought an exquisite pair of diamond earrings for Maya, and Seema bought a matching chain and pendant in white gold.

When they returned home and presented their mother with the gifts, she was deeply moved. It had been years since she'd been gifted jewellery. "You two should not have spent so much money on me!"

"Amma, we haven't seen you wear jewellery since we were children. It's for us as much as for you. We knew you couldn't refuse it from us," said Salman and Seema, one after the other.

"But you have to save up for your marriages. Why are you wasting your money on me?"

"We do not think we will get married any time soon."

"It is all Allah's wish, whenever your wedding flower blooms your marriage will take place."

"Amma, you and your fantasies."

"Well, as I always say, marriage is in your destiny, but do make an effort."

Salman and Seema looked at Maya with infinite love as she put on the earrings and chain.

The monsoon breeze was moist and refreshing the next morning. The strong fragrance of hasna hena flowers had kept Maya in a restless sleep. As she came out to the veranda, she saw the shefali flowers spread out their virgin white and orange carpet on the stairway. Her backyard kadam flowers were dancing in mirth at the caress of the first morning rain shower, and she felt at peace. Her battles were over, and she had no more expectations from life.

In the afternoon, a letter came for her father-in-law. A letter from Modhu. He had had a heart attack the night before; his burial was today.

Maya sat down in her favourite easy chair. The rain had left a crispness in the air. Nothing in life surprised her anymore. The years of her childhood flashed before her eyes. Then adulthood. Then the five years of bliss with Modhu, the raising of her children in his absence. She could have remarried if her faith had not been shattered. She was not bitter. Just tired, maybe sad. She felt no resentment.

Her father-in-law entered her room and gently put his hand on her head.

"There is something you need to do, my dear daughter." He had always addressed her as such. Never daughter-in-law. He wanted Maya and his grandchildren to live with him and his wife. Modhu had promised his father he would never come to his house as long as his parents visited him and his second wife and children twice during the Eid holidays. This arrangement had worked out well.

"Yes, father, please sit down."

"Modhu left me a letter as you know. It was dated thirty days before his death."

"Father, I do not need to know anything about that letter. It must be personal, and I am not interested."

"There is something important that he wrote before he died, and it concerns you."

"Father, there is nothing that binds us together anymore and I do not think he needed to make any communication with me before or after his death."

"Dear, his spirit has departed. There is no need for any kind of bitterness."

"That has been a closed chapter for me for a long time, and I do not want to reopen it."

"Maya, I have to inform you about this because it concerns you."

"I do not think there is anything about your son, dead or alive, that could concern me."

"Maya, you know I never brought up my son's name in your presence for the last twenty years, but now it is absolutely necessary that I convey to you his last wish."

"What is the point? I know my answer to any request that you or he might make. So, what is the point?" Maya was becoming extremely impatient and irritated. A touch of steel crept into her voice.

"Believe me, after I read out my son's last wish you might change your mind. It is my request."

"If it is your request to me father, I respect that."

"Listen, Maya, there is not much time. His dead body is being brought to this house."

"Why is his body being brought here?" Maya felt a numbness creeping into her hands and feet. She tried to calm herself, to imagine the unending golden beach and blue frothing waves of Cox's Bazar, the picturesque, pristine forest beside the beach, but images of her ex-husband dominated. The numbness was gradually winging its way into her heart.

Her eyes were dry but burning. She took grip of her increasing pain and looked at her father-in-law. He seemed so distant. Like the indistinct curves of television pictures when the frequency was lost. He was agitated but trying to calm himself. He was speaking but she could not hear him. She tried to control herself.

"As I was saying, this was his last wish. Modhu expressed in his letter that he had left instructions that after his body has been washed according to the Muslim religious rites and shrouded with two pieces of new, white, non-stitched cloths, it should be brought to our front courtyard so that you can have a last look before he is buried."

"What!" Maya could not believe what she was hearing.

"Yes, this was his last wish. That you should see his face one last time."

"How dare he!"

Her father-in-law was sobbing uncontrollably. "Modhu's body will be here any minute now. Please Maya, can you dress in a white sari and come out when the body arrives?"

There was a huge commotion outside the house. Modhu's purified body had arrived. In somber tones, the Arabic Surahs of the Holy Quran were being recited by relatives and friends of the family. The strong fragrance of incense wafted in dense smoke around the body. Modhu's mother was sticking the incense in clusters in cups of rice to hold them straight. She was so irritated and angry that she could not find the brass incense stick holders bought specifically for this occasion.

It was time to take the body to be buried in the family graveyard, but everyone was waiting in apprehension for Maya to come out and see Modhu's face for the last time. The afternoon Asr prayers were completed, and before the sun set and heralded the time for Maghreb prayers, the body must be buried. The priests were getting impatient. Modhu's mother ran quickly to Maya's room. Maya was sitting on her bed, unchanged and unwashed.

"Maya! Why have you not changed and why have you not performed your ablution?"

Maya stared at her mother-in-law with cold, unfeeling eyes. Her entire body was grasped in iciness.

"Why, mother, why should I change into a white sari now?"

"What do you mean?"

"My life has been completely white and a blank slate since Modhu left me twenty years ago. Why should I wear a white sari now? To prove what?"

"Okay, Maya, you do not have to change. Just go and see his face for the last time. The time is flying, and we need to bury his body as soon as possible to avoid further pain to the departed soul."

"I am not seeing his face," said Maya.

Modhu's mother could not accept what she heard. "What do you mean by that? Please, Maya, I know it is very hard for you, but please do not be stubborn."

"Amma, I am not being stubborn. I am doing what is the natural course for me."

"There is no time for your dramatics now!" wailed Modhu's mother. "Everyone is waiting..."

"I am not a drama queen, you know very well, Amma."

"Then what is your problem?"

"There is absolutely no problem with me. You can go ahead and bury him. He can be buried without his last wish being fulfilled!"

"Maya, do you really mean that?"

"Amma, I have sacrificed countless dreams and wishes for the last twenty years. He can sacrifice one of his wishes, even if he's dead."

HER PINK PEARLS

New York felt different this time. As Ayesha left the airport, she carried with her a new kind of loneliness. The gold-plated orchid and matching pendant, supposedly made from fresh orchids, that Pam had given her at her layover in Thailand were tucked away snugly in her handbag. Memories of Bangladesh started to fade while she thought about the days ahead. There was the monotony of work: five days a week packing the slaughtered chickens with blood-stained plastic gloves. Then there were the house chores: grocery shopping, cooking three meals a day, laundry and cleaning on the weekend. Days in New York were duty without pleasure and seemed relentless in their demands. It wasn't just the slog that irked Ayesha. It was her mother-in-law and, perhaps worse these days, her husband, Kamal. Life here with them had begun two decades ago and had devolved into a bad dream, a cheap stereotype.

She'd thought visiting Bangladesh would rejuvenate her. And in a way, it had — while she was there, at least. The effects were fading with each kilometre the cabbie put between her and the airport. Convincing Kamal to let her go was hard. Convincing her mother-in-law Rahima was even harder. She loved the old lady but couldn't bear the constant reminders of her childlessness. Did her mother-in-law not think she pined for children too? Did Rahima not know how she ached, how she longed for just that? It seemed an unfair point to bully her on. Often when Rahima was droning on about the absence of children, Ayesha felt as if her whole being sighed. She longed to hold some tender little thing to her chest, to sing lullabies to it, feel its warmth, its heartbeat. It would be marvellous to hear the ancient word *mother* called out to her with infinite, unconditional love from her own child. Her efforts would be worth something then. Her suffering would not be in vain. If Allah blessed her with a child, she promised to go to the grave of Khwaja Moinuddin Chishti of Ajmer in India and offer a gold covering quilt for his tomb, following tradition that had been passed down to Ayesha and others in her society from their ancestors. While there she would add rice and meat to the giant copper pot to be cooked and fed to hundreds of destitute people. She also promised the Almighty Above that she would sacrifice two goats in Dhaka and feed the orphanage children biryani with the sacrificial meat.

Marriage hadn't turned out the way Ayesha imagined. Kamal was handsome, well-spoken and seemed tender at first. However, once the nerves and newness of marriage wore off, things began to slide. The routine of daily life took hold and Kamal settled himself all too naturally into a state of self-interest. He handled the money she brought home, leaving her a nominal amount for her shopping and necessities and then complaining when meals weren't feasts. He was content to watch television all day, stay out late doing who-knew-what, only to come home blindly groping through the darkened bedroom for what he considered his property, his wife. Any tenderness Kamal had exhibited in the first few months of marriage, any gratitude or generosity, were gone now. In their place were animalism, greed and an overall disregard for the feelings of the woman he married. It would have been different had there been children, perhaps, but Ayesha couldn't entertain such what-ifs. They were painful, impossible.

That was where the pink pearls came in. Ayesha had given up any hope of Kamal changing. She resigned herself to the subjugation of this life, telling herself that at least if she received a token, a single symbolic manifestation of her worth, perhaps this whole ordeal could be endured. The token she settled her desire on was a string of pink pearls. She'd first seen them five years ago in Canada. Kamal's sister wore them with a matching pair of drop earrings. Kamal's sister was the lady of her household, respected and loved by her children and by her husband, and the more Ayesha witnessed her going about her days in confidence and contentment, the more she began to associate those pink peals with her worth, her happiness. It was Ayesha's birthday soon, and she'd made sure to point out the pearls to Kamal, to let him know how important they were to her, how desirous of them she was. She'd even gone so far as to tell him flat-out once or twice that she would like a string of her own for her birthday. She believed that the pearls would infuse her with the life she wanted, or at least would make her feel as though she had it.

Ayesha brushed away her tears. Kamal drove taxi but hadn't come to the airport to pick her up for reasons she couldn't recall. She couldn't afford the taxi she sat in now, but couldn't manage her luggage on the bus by herself. Her knees ached. Plane journeys with their cramped spaces aggravated her osteoarthritis, and the smell of the recirculated air inside the plane was nauseating. She hoped her mother-in-law would like the silk sari and woolen shawl that she'd bought in Kolkata. Her West Bengali friends living in Brooklyn had told her to go to Gariahat for cheap rates on saris, shawls and shalwar-kameezes. She had paid a bit more than was in her budget for a particularly special sari because she felt Kamal's mother would love it, and the matching embroidered shawl was a hundred percent lightweight pashmina wool.

Back in India, as she walked the streets of Gariahat towards the tram line to go back to the hotel, she saw a mother and her teenage daughter sitting on low, coloured cane moras. It was a warm day with a light breeze, the sort that made one feel as though everything, no matter how desolate life seemed, would be okay. The mother and daughter seemed to feel this way as they sat there, hands outstretched, while a man knelt before them applying ornate patterns of henna. Ayesha had never seen a male henna artist on the roadside, even in the streets of old Dhaka in Bangladesh. It struck her enough that she felt compelled to stop and investigate.

"Do you do feet as well?" she asked the artist.

"Yes, Mem Saheb, we do. Any design, just choose from here."

The man handed Ayesha a book of exquisite designs. Out of all the flowers, birds, and butterflies, Ayesha selected a lotus. A fully blossomed lotus with a bud and leaf.

"I can only pay you one hundred taka for each foot. Is that okay?"

"Yes, Mem Saheb, I will do it. It is perfectly okay."

Ayesha spread out her bare feet in total abandon as the artist applied her selected symbol. As he neared completion of the design, the man said, "You did a good thing choosing the lotus, Didi. It's a good symbol to have a lotus on one's feet. It symbolizes integrity, trust and purity."

Ayesha loved her lotus and its meaning so much that she decided to pay double the offered amount. She also felt immense sympathy and pity for the artist, whose only means of income were henna designs and the tips that came from it. As Ayesha sat on the little cane mora, she wanted to know a bit more about henna culture in Kolkata, so she struck up a conversation with the mother and daughter who still sat nearby enjoying their new adornment.

"Are you going to a wedding?" she asked them.

"Yes, my brother's daughter's wedding," said the mother, who was wearing a red-and-white checkered cotton sari.

"Are there not beauty parlours where one could do the same henna? I believe there is a Shomi's Glamour World branch in Goriahat who could do it?"

"Yes, of course there is, but the price will be triple there."

The daughter added, "My Ma said that if I save that money, she will put it towards my sari."

"And there is no difference between the pattern and colour here. So why should I throw my money down the drain?"

Ayesha smiled, told the mother and daughter that their henna looked beautiful and thanked them for entertaining her enquiries.

She thought of her own wedding, the optimistic way in which she'd adorned herself, the thrill of what was to come — what she had hoped was to come.

The artist took her sandals and helped her get a taxi to the hotel. Her henna or mehdi had not completely dried, so the journey had to be made barefoot. As she entered the hotel lobby with her hennaed feet, sandals in hand, the Bengali-Chinese receptionist, wearing an exquisite Nakshi Kantha–designed Murshidabad silk sari made by the tribal girls at Shantiniketon, gave her a knowing smile. It was as if, in that moment, the two women shared a secret knowledge of the air of freedom Ayesha's afternoon held, of the indulgence and symbolism of her freshly painted lotus.

Kamal had just woken up and was eating breakfast when she arrived home. He gave her a pleasant smile and got up to help her with the luggage. His mother was busy frying parathas, as well as aloo bhaji and bhuna gosht, and chomchom for dessert. The scent of ghee filled the room.

"How is everyone back home? Did you keep well and get to eat all your favourite foods?" Kamal asked in a routine sort of way.

Ayesha took a seat beside him. "The trip was just what I needed. Everyone is well. The food, as always, was exquisite."

"Did you manage to go to Kolkata?"

"Yes, but Fatima could not go with me. I went alone."

"Alone?"

"Yes, what's the harm? I know it well."

Ayesha took a paratha and glanced up to catch a sour stare from her mother-in-law. "Why don't you let Kamal eat first?" Rahima said.

Her mother-in-law subscribed to systems of the old days in Bangladesh. There, men eat first, and when they are finished, women clear the men's plates before sitting down to feed themselves. Rahima had been cooking and feeding Kamal for weeks while Ayesha was away and wore her exhaustion with animated exaggeration. Rahima had moved to New York to live with them years ago, after her husband died, and seemed to resent the small spaces and forward-thinking ways.

Ayesha was jet-lagged and did not want to get into a conflict on her first day back. She said nothing to her mother-in-law; she was feeling full anyway. It would be best to shower and sleep a few hours before getting her clothes and lunch ready for work the next morning. As she stood up, Kamal pulled her hand from under the table. He wanted to join her for the shower, but she was in no mood for that. Her energy was drained. She looked at him and shook her head. He scowled and angrily pushed his plate away. If she knew him to be faithful, things might have been different. She might have felt more inclined to entertain his desires.

But she knew better.

It was one Friday last year when she'd gone to Jackson Heights to get halal beef for some guests coming over for the weekend that she'd first caught him. Jackson Heights was the Little Bangladesh of New York, an attraction for all Bangladeshis living abroad and could be compared to the Danforth and Victoria Park of Toronto, which were known as the Little Bangladesh of Canada. There were Bangladeshi grocers selling fruits, vegetables, fish, spices, snacks and sweet meats. There were also Bangladeshi restaurants catering to demands for Bengali biryani, rice and fish combos, bhajees and bhortas. Cooked and uncooked dry fish were specialties. Kamal liked the moghlai kachhi biryani made with mutton and potatoes on Friday afternoons at Aladdin's. Ayesha had checked the time and, realizing it was almost 2 p.m., when Kamal took his break, had peeked into Aladdin's and seen Kamal eating biryani with an almond-eyed, black-haired beauty she'd seen around a few times before. They were sitting close, touching knees, and Kamal was putting a spoonful of biryani into her mouth. The two of them smiled like dumb teenagers, and Ayesha, upon seeing them, fled the scene like a burglar.

There were others. Some she knew, some she did not. She found lipstick on his clothing, smelled perfumes that weren't hers, saw him again on occasion, cozy in a booth with one woman or another. Always smiling, always touching. She confronted him once and was met with a shrug and brush of the hand. He didn't even care enough to protest. Often, she wished she had the courage to divorce him, imagining what life alone would be like, how free, how easy, how painless.

It was two days after she returned from her trip that Ayesha returned from shopping to find an empty house. It was after seven and Kamal should have been there waiting, as was his habit, for dinner. Ayesha wondered if he might be at one of the debates. He was constantly engaged in local politics, and it was common for men to attend debates while their wives shopped.

There were groups from the Awami League Party, who were in power in Bangladesh, and the Bangladesh Nationalist Party, who were in opposition, which led to heated discussions.

Sometimes, arguments stopped just shy of fist-fights.

Ayesha resolved to pay no mind for the time being and set up the table for herself and her mother-in-law. Rahima seemed happy as she ate, perhaps relieved that she was no longer obliged to cook. After dinner, over tea and rice cakes that she had brought over from Dhaka, Ayesha decided to present the gifts she'd picked out for her mother-in-law in Kolkata. Rahima obviously hadn't been expecting gifts. She revealed a deep smile as she received her sari and shawl, but soon caught herself, as if participating in some outlawed activity, and returned to her usual scowl.

"There was no need for any gifts for me. I am an old woman who has nothing to look forward to anymore. Not even the hope of a grandchild," Rahima said.

"Well," Ayesha tried, "do you like them, at least?"

"You should not have spent money on me." She looked again at her new sari. "The colours are nice."

Ayesha was sound asleep when Kamal returned from wherever he had been.

She pretended to be asleep while he undressed and climbed into bed. His hands began to run over her body, his beer-breath hot at the back of her neck.

"I have work tomorrow morning. You know I need my sleep," she said, still half-asleep but giving up at the game of pretending.

"Won't take long, I promise."

He was already on top of her, grunting loudly as he sucked and bit her nipples. He pushed himself in quickly and with force. She swallowed her protest. It would only make things worse. She'd learned from decades of marriage that he would eventually have what he wanted one way or another. And if he was half-awake at dawn when she got up to take her shower, he would do it again.

After he finished and rolled over, falling swiftly into a noisy sleep, she thought of how much she would have loved it if he had instead held her and told her that he had missed her while she was gone, asked her how she was feeling, what she needed. She remembered her college logic professor who repeatedly emphasized that the only difference between humans and animals was the fact that the former possessed rationalism. However, Kamal's behaviour did not exude any form of rationalism or empathy.

Ayesha's mood went from hopeless to ecstatic the next morning when she found a receipt in the pocket of Kamal's pants. Even the usually dismal bell at the factory had a kind of sweetness to it now. The receipt she'd found was for the very pink pearl necklace she longed for. Suddenly the way she felt about her husband shifted; he did care, he did listen. He was just bad at showing it, and this pearl necklace was his way of letting her know she mattered to him. She now felt that she had been rather harsh and decided to make it up to him tonight by putting on her nicest sari, some extra eyeliner, and greeting him in bed the way she had when they were first married.

As she clocked out at the factory, Ayesha remembered that she had to drop off medication for her uncle who lived across town. She took two buses and one subway out of her usual route home to get there. It was already getting dark and she would have to rush home to serve dinner to Rahima. The day had been busy. She'd skipped her own lunch and was hungry beyond words before she even got to her uncle's.

As Ayesha stepped off of the second bus and headed for the subway station, she tried to control her hunger and dizziness. She glanced at the open space of a park where a mother was breastfeeding her child under a tree. Nearby, a couple was embracing. She stopped in her tracks. She could not see their faces but recognized the man's jacket. The jacket she had purchased for Kamal from Raymond's in Kolkata. Yes, it was him under a lamp in the half-lit corner of the park, a few yards away from the breastfeeding woman. The girl in his arms had a sleeveless little black dress on. Her face was turned towards Kamal. The dress had a deep neckline, and half her breasts popped out because of her push-up bra. Ayesha couldn't pry her eyes from the woman, first from her plunging neckline, then from the string of pearls nestled elegantly there. Pink pearls. Her pink pearls. Her body went hot.

She left the scene, continued to her uncle's and then went home with the calm of one still in shock.

Her mother-in-law must have heard her near the door, for before Ayesha could turn her key in the lock, Rahima swung the door open and stood there like a blazing Goddess Durga.

"So, my lady returns at last. Were you out so late with your new lover?"

"Of course not, mother," Ayesha said with an eerie calm.

She stood there glaring at Rahima in shocked silence.

Rahima Begum said, "Let Kamal come home tonight. I'll put a full stop to all of your affairs."

"Are you calling me a liar?'

"I am. And I will a hundred times. You are a rotten female who doesn't care about her husband. There is no place for such a female in *my* house."

Ayesha smirked. She calmly entered the kitchen and picked out her favourite knife from the slab, the one she'd always preferred for its convenient grip.

With an otherworldly swiftness, Ayesha swung her mother-in-law to the floor. She felt she was the most powerful figure in this world. She sat cross-legged on Rahima's body and stabbed her in the chest repeatedly. As the blood spilled over her body and face, Ayesha became stronger. It was as if the blood was the elixir of life and was rejuvenating her body and soul. She felt emancipated. Enlightened.

The golden flash of rage gradually disappeared as she felt Rahima go limp. Ayesha had never felt so free and independent in her whole life. She was newly birthed, ready to conquer whatever challenge the world threw at her. She slowly got up and went to grab her cellphone. She dialed the police and waited, hovering over the old woman's chest. The space between action and consequence seemed endless, and in that space, Ayesha began to calm.

The chemicals that once coursed through her dissipated, and where once the blood had seemed like red peals of emancipation, it was now just blood, dirty and dank. Everything was wrong. She removed her socks, pulled her feet into view over the woman's throat, and saw the lotus there, still bold, a crimson symbol of loyalty, of transformation. She began to weep, and when the police arrived, she collapsed into the officer's chest with a speechlessness that would never clear.

OF FOX AND FIDDLE

Aakash: I am the fox, you are the fiddle.

Shona: Why do you say that?

A: You are the love of my life, and I am yours for eternity. I am the green-eyed fox, and you are the melody of my life.

S: But it is the twilight of my life. Why did you not come into my life when there was daylight, when the flowers of my heart had not wilted?

A: Paagla hawar badal deene. This insane wind on this monsoon day.

S: You are so ambiguous sometimes.

A: Until you came along, I never knew the meaning of love. I have found my soulmate now and I am fulfilled.

S: You are my boundless sky, and I am your limitless sea.

A: You are composing poetry yet you yourself are the lines of my poetry.

S: I am your unwritten poetry, your unfinished dreams.

A: As Pablo Neruda said, "I will do to you what spring does to the cherry trees."

S: I would like to live in those eyes of yours, which are pools of unlimited knowledge.

A: You are my Muse; I do not need anything else.

S: The very first day that I am going to meet you, I would like to plant my first kiss on the palm of your right hand. The hand which creates such immortal lines of prose and poetry.

A: The very first day that I envision you there will be a tornado!

S: Without touching?

A: How can that happen without touching, my angel?

S: Ours is a spiritual and intellectual union, primarily.

A: I would like to drown myself in your pristine forest, in the world of your sweet cherries, in the honey and nectar of your sexy lips! In the jungle of your fragrant tresses!

S: I am not meeting you then, alone.

A: Are you stupid? How can we make love in front of people?

S: Why do we have to make love the very first day that we meet? Do we not have our entire lives?

A: My Shona, why are you acting like a child?

S: My Aakash, why are you so impatient?

A: Okay, let nature take its course. Would you agree to that?

S: In other words, leave it to nature?

A: Shona, try to understand, I am a human being, and I will be meeting my Love Goddess for the first time in my life.

S: Your next line will be that you are a man of flesh and blood and that I am a stone-hearted mortal, right?

A: Shona, look at the monsoon rain outside your window. Your sky is shedding tears for you...

S: Do not try to distract me, Aakash.

A: Okay, my darling Shona. I'll condition myself to abstinence.

S (singing): Tumi aashbe bole / Kache daakbe bole / Bhalobashbe ogo shudhu moreh...

Because you will be coming / Because you will call me closer / Because you will only love me...

A (singing): Because I will be coming / I will call you to come to me / I will love you only...

S (singing): Tai champa bokul / Kore gondhe aakul, / Ei jotsna raate moneh porhe...

That is why the fragrance of the champa and bokul reminds me of you this moonlit night...

A (singing): That is why the fragrance of the champa and bokul reminds me of you on this moonlit night...

S: I yearn for thy lips.

A: No, abstinence is the law, my lady.

S: Alright, if that's the way you want it, Your Royal Highness!

A: I did not want it, you are the one who wanted it, my lady! I am just following your orders.

S: I do not understand men. Ours will be an arranged marriage. Don't we need time to get to know each other before we jump into a physical relationship?

A: We have been doing that for the last year. I know everything about your soul and body.

S: Soul, yes, but body?

A: Do you want me to describe your physique?

S: Poet, you have never met me, never laid eyes on my body, how can you describe me?

A: My Muse, I can describe everything about you, mentally and physically.

S: Now, wait a minute!

A: I can wait for eternity to get to know you, but what more can you learn when you know someone for eternity?

S: I think your animalism is taking over your rationalism. Sometimes I don't understand you at all.

A: We should all go back to the medieval times.

S: Then how would you write this?

A: I wish I was born in the stone age.

S: Okay, I give up. I don't know if I want to go through with this marriage business.

A: Living together would be better in my opinion.

S: Better for you or me?

A: Better for mankind.

S: Do you think I should start working on a new novel?

A: Yes, Shona. Write a novel about us.

S: Sometimes the margin between imagination and reality is so fine that one merges into the other and the reader no longer knows where the writer stands.

A: I did not read Salman Rushdie's *The Satanic Verses*, but I heard that was the problem with it. The readers could not differentiate between truth and fiction.

S: Even if they did, Rushdie should be totally condemned because I believe that a writer does have the freedom to think and write as long as he does not step on someone else's toes. I hate him with a passion.

A: Yes, he has irreparably hurt the sensibilities of the Muslims all over the world.

S: Should I write a novel or a collection of short stories?

A: I love your poetry. Why don't you do an anthology of English poems?

S: Boro Apa said very few people read poetry nowadays.

A: She also said the number of people reading books has decreased worldwide.

S: I told Daisy to read Khaled Hosseini's *The Kite Runner*. She started it, but when the movie came out she saw it. Now, she is not finishing the book. I loved reading it so much!

A: You did the same with Rushdie's *Midnight's Children*. I loved reading that book, but instead of finishing it, you ran to see the movie.

S: You did the same also with Michael Ondaatje's *The English Patient*.

A: Well, that film got the Oscar for that year, and I loved seeing it, especially the love scenes.

S: But you missed the charm of the book.

A: The scenes of the electrifying lovemaking was worth it!

S: I guess, in this world and time, the majority of people are more into movies, television, talking books and stage shows than reading. People do not have the time to read anymore.

A: Did you read any of Alice Munro's short stories after she got the Nobel Prize for Literature?

S: Yes, I did, and I loved them. She is so spontaneous, straightforward, simple and effective. She writes so beautifully about the day-to-day happenings of ordinary people so elegantly that it achieves extraordinary standards.

A: She brought short stories into an altogether different height. She said that she did not write short stories to pass away her time until she writes a novel.

S: The day that the award was announced, the CBC had some quotations of hers all over the hourly news.

A: Which one caught your eye?

S: "When a man leaves a room, he leaves everything behind him. When a woman leaves a room, she takes everything with her outside the room."

A: Do you know why she said that?

S: I understand where she was coming from.

A: Because when a man leaves a room, he knows he will come back to that room.

S: I must share what you just said with my friends.

A: As long as you do not share me with your friends.

S: I would like to donate you to my friends.

A: You are stuck with me for life. Ours will be an infallible bond.

S: Did you hear about Robin Williams?

A: Yes.

S: He made everyone laugh yet was so sad himself.

A: Who could have imagined that he suffered so much?

S: Not I.

A: Can you imagine, Shona, he is a famous star today, but only a legend tomorrow?

S: Sometimes a great personality, an immortal creation by mankind, a miracle of nature or a piece of prose or poetry creates a magic that is forever embedded in your heart.

A: The Taj Mahal versus the Niagara Falls, the wonder of nature as opposed to the immortality of love created by the human race.

S: I feel like eating green tea-flavoured ice cream.

A: Come Shona, come to me and I will treat you to the best ice cream in town.

S: You always turn a simple thing into something erotic.

A: My darling, you have only seen the tip of the iceberg.

S: I do not have any intention of seeing the rest of you or the rest of the iceberg.

A: See sweetheart, now you are the one grazing on eroticism.

S: Of course not!

A: Do you remember what Freud said about the human mind?

S: I do not remember, nor do I want to remember.

A: I am just counting the days to our Nikkah and then my Shona, I will teach you Freud and more.

S: There is still time to change my mind about this marriage.

A: Even if there is time and you try your best, my dearest Shona, you cannot let me go or escape from the landscapes of my love.

S: My Aakash, please do not say such silly things.

A: My Shona, I will travel with you to the doors of the seven heavens and make you taste the honey and ambrosia of a perfect union.

S: Aakash, please be patient.

A: I have crossed all the seven seas of my patience.

S: Sometimes I think all men are the same. All other boundaries are transcended because of this physical thing.

A: What is life without this ultimate pleasure?

S: I thought our dream was to go to the highest mountaintop with our favourite books and discover each other through browsing and reading.

A: That plan, of course, is still unchanged, Your Royal Highness.

S: But my lord, I feel you are straying from our dreams.

A: Dreams can be of many kinds, my lady.

S: My lord, I dream of a life together with you on the golden sand of life's seashore, where the blue sky meets the blue waves, where the sun never sets and the moon never fades, and where the twinkling stars sprinkle their dust on our contented bodies and souls. Where our free spirits will effortlessly glide up amidst the fragrant Falguni breeze.

A: I dream of my new bride, the most beautiful and elegant partner a man can imagine by his side. A soulmate, companion and beloved wife wearing a red Banarasi silk sari with molten gold border, a red bindi, gold nose ring and a pair of gold anklets with little bells on your hennaed feet so that my heart lights up every time I hear those bells as you come close to me.

S: There is a difference between the material and the immaterial, the tangible and the intangible, the value of things and the priceless things in life.

A: Have you ever wondered why I am marrying so late in life?

S: Have you ever wondered why I did not agree to marry anyone before?

A: We waited for each other, we never found anyone else, we are made for each other?

S: No, no and no. How tacky, like a Hindi movie!

A: Shona, stop it. You accept it or not, it is the ultimate truth.

S: Sometimes you are so dramatic and so like a teenager.

A: Listen my Goddess, this is the simple and ultimate truth. We are made for each other.

S: Your Royal Highness, no one can change anything inside your Royal head.

A: Remember you said that for you are coming into this Royal household and I love thee my Queen.

S: I once heard a radio interview of many times award-winning actress Suchitra Sen on Akaashbani Kolkata radio. I asked her director to mention a memorable incident regarding her and I was amazed at his observation.

A: My Queen, when you come to my kingdom you will be amazed beyond your wildest imagination at the surprises I have in store for you.

S: When I enter the hamlet of your heart, I will cuddle up and go into my world of dreams.

A: I love your lingering fragrance on me.

S: For now, can I continue with Suchitra Sen?

A: When did I stop you?

S: The director said that once he was instructing Suchitra for a melancholy scene and told her to cry after her dialogue, she asked him, "Should I keep the tears inside my eyes or let them spill out?"

A: The only condition that I will give you after our marriage is that I never want to see even the hint of tears in the beautiful expanse of your eyes.

S: Why do you have such a one-track mind? This world is not only about you.

A: My world is you, about you and only about you, my Shona.

S: As Rumi said, "Lovers don't finally meet somewhere. They're in each other all along."

A: Kahlil Gibran once said, "If you love somebody, let them go, for if they return, they were always yours. And if they don't, they never were." Whatever he said, I don't care Shona, although he is one of my favourites, I can never let you go to wait and see what happens.

S: Why not experiment?

A: I will die in the meantime!

S: Gibran also said, "Out of suffering have emerged the strongest souls, the most massive characters are seared with scars."

A: I am a strong enough soul, I do not need any more suffering, especially if it means being separated from the love of my life.

S: I have to go back to T.S. Elliot, "Only those who will risk going too far can possibly find out how far one can go."

A: Excuse me, I am not that adventurous.

S: I believe, if you are a true romantic and lover, you do have to be adventurous.

A: Come on, Shona, have mercy on this love-deprived soul.

S: My Aakash, when did I deprive you of anything?

A: Every time I want to light the fire of our love, you pour water on it.

S: Love transcends the physical hills and valleys and derives its fragrance and enhancement from the soul and spirit.

A: You mean to say I do not have a heart? I only have physical demands?

S: I do not mean to say anything. You just said it yourself.

A: Shona, you are so cruel sometimes.

S: Cleanse your heart of all impurities and inject new blood that will rejuvenate your thoughts and emotions. Do Yoga, attain Nirvana.

A: If I really go into meditation, you will be the one who will cry for my love.

S: Let us go into meditation together after celebrating our first wedding anniversary.

A: Will you become tired of me so soon after marriage?

S: I will never be tired of you, with or without marriage.

A: I wish I could live with you beside the sea, make love to you morning and evening when the sun breaks at dawn and sets at dusk and under the stars.

S: What would we do for food? And for our living?

A: We will write poetry and read them out to each other and catch and cook and eat the fishes whenever we are hungry.

S: Life was simple like that once upon a time.

A: It could again be like that if people forgot about wars, weapons, boundaries, race, religion, wealth and ownership.

S: If the present universe gets annihilated and we all start anew.

A: If all the children of this planet start fresh and do not listen to their fathers and forefathers.

S: It is such a small life but such ado over everything.

A: Let us all make a simple promise and start a new life.

S: A life where there will be no jealousy, hatred, murder, suicide, anger, bitterness and regret.

A: Many have spoken about this New Beginning, but few fulfill it.

S: I like this serious side of yours. I can imagine your face attaining that level where you are concentrating on something so sensitive that your forehead has those wrinkled lines and your eyes become dark pools of rebellion.

A: Wow! You do have a vivid imagination and correct analysis, although I cannot see myself thus.

S: Aakash dearest, I do know you so well now. Like the palm of my right hand.

A: You are part of me now and every time I hang up the phone with you I feel part of me is stripped away.

S: Aaaaaa.

A: Shona, please take me seriously. I will never let you shed a single teardrop for me or anything in our lives... Eternal happiness will be ours if we speak our minds to each other.

S: Okay, let me give you a long line-up of where you have to take me after our marriage, or my next teardrop will certainly spill out.

A: I didn't know I would be obliged to do that.

S: Your bachelor days will be over, and you do have to sacrifice your time and coordinate your priorities with mine for the marriage to work.

A: Yes, my lady.

S: I would love it if you took me to the Rash Festival of the Monipuri Tribe, the Fair of the Nude Pagla at Gopalganj, the Baul Mela, the cockfights, bull fights, Jabbarer Boli Khela, the kite-flying festival and, last but not the least, Bou Mela or the Fair for Married Women.

A: I never heard about any special fair for married women.

S: It is actually a fair mostly observed by the Hindu women folk where an ancient banyan tree is associated with the Goddess Kali. This old tree with its roots and branches is compared to a woman's hair, and this festival takes place on the first day of the Bengali new year, the month of Baisakh. Married and unmarried women from the Sonargaon village, as well as from other villages, come and offer Prasad or offerings to the Goddess in the form of sweets, rice cakes and seasonal fruits and ask for a better and successful future for themselves and their families.

A: I would like you to take me to the Wangala Festival of the Garos, Poush Mela, Nabanno Utsab and Basanta Utsab.

S: Your list is small compared to mine.

A: I have not yet finished my list. The rest I will demand on my wedding night, my precious Shona.

S: You and your one-track mind! Give me a hint of the rest of your list.

A: And spoil the surprise?

S: Sometimes you really frustrate me.

A: Shona, I will let you cross that bridge when you come to it.

S: I have to hang up now, my dearest Aakash. I am so sleepy and tired, I don't understand how it got so late.

A: It will always be like this sweetheart, when we are married and sit down together to talk, and you know, when I hold you in my arms you will not know how the time will fly.

S: If you promise to treat me to a cup of frozen green tea every day in the summer.

A: Of course, I will, and you will let me do whatever I want?

S: For now, go to sleep.

A: I will only go to sleep if you promise me to come in my dreams and hold me to your bosom and never let me go. I want to wake up with your lingering fragrance all over me and the marks of my love all over you.

S: I liked the first part of your imagination but not the second part. You are absolutely shameless.

A: Okay, my Queen let us call it a night.

S: Yes, my lord as you say.

A: Remember, always as I say. Today and tomorrow.

S: If you order me around like that, I am not going to marry you. Everything between us is fifty-fifty, Your Royal Highness.

A: Goodnight, my lady, my precious one, my dearest angel. Whatever your conditions, I humbly accept.

S: Goodnight, my lord. I will be very fair at all times and our union will be made in Heaven and showered with eternal bliss.

A: And if life's clouds burden us at times, we will enjoy the rainfall after our trials and errors.

Acknowledgements

My first and foremost gratitude and literary debt is to **Robin Richardson**, award-winning poet and author, public speaker and Spiritual Advisor. My daughter Fariah attended high school with her and when I sought an editor who was also a poet, who would do justice to my short stories, I struck gold with Robin! The brilliant and ever-inspiring Robin advised, guided and helped me through every step of the way. Being a poet myself, I often leave some reflections and lyrics unwritten, like poetry. She not only understood my vision but loved my unwritten reflections. She also moved me with her exceptional understanding, expertise and love.

I am absolutely indebted to my University of Dhaka Professor **Dr. Habib Zafarullah**, who currently resides in Australia. He was visiting Toronto a few years ago and advised me to write short stories with specific issues that needed to be addressed openly. I have three volumes of Bengali short stories, but this is my first attempt at English short stories. I hope I can do justice to the vision he had for me. Thank you, Professor Zafarullah, for believing in me and encouraging me.

My niece **Esha** travelled on this journey with me, every step of the way, from the beginning to the end. She advised me and helped me perfect my stories to best represent the cultural contexts of both Bangladesh and Canada. Her utmost patience, immense selflessness, constant smile, unconditional love and golden heart has won me over for life.

Last, but not the least I am infinitely grateful to my precious late daughter, **Fariah**. She was thirty-five years old and thirty-six weeks pregnant with her unborn child and has left behind a first-born, a two-year-old baby boy. She was an academic, an activist and an educator. She was my editor, advisor, critic and the reviewer of many books of mine. She was my best friend in this world. I visualized the reflections of my dreams in her eyes. I understood her like none other and taught her to unwind her wings to fly amidst the endless expanse of the blue sky, for which she always expressed gratitude. She won a place in the hearts of everyone around her with her love, patience, care, warmth and dedication for humanity. May she rest in eternal peace. Angel, this book would not see the light if you were not constantly beside me.

Rummana Chowdhury is the author of forty-seven books, both in Bengali and English, comprising poetry, short stories, columns, novels and analytical essays. Rummana was Bangladesh's national badminton champion from 1975 to 1978. She excelled academically and was also nationally acclaimed as a leading debate commentator, radio and TV talk show host and recitation leader.

Today, she has become a leading global commentator on issues of migration that pertain to the South Asian Diaspora, violence against women, Diaspora literature, translation, cultural and historical remembrance strategies and feminist politics and culture. Rummana has received several notable awards, including Meritorious Service 1977 (RCMP of Canada,) the Ontario Volunteers Award 2000, Woman of the Year 2010 (Canada) and Writer and Translator 2016 (Ontario Bengali Cultural Society). She has also received several awards for her contributions to Bengali, English and Diaspora literature and her translation work from Bangladesh, India, Europe and North America. These include the International Michael Modhu Sudan Datta Literary Award 2014, the Sunil Gangopaddhyay Literary Award 2017, the Bangladesh

Lekhika Sangha Award for Literature and Translation 2017 and the Kobi Jasim Uddin Gold Medal 2019, among others.

Rummana has been working as an accredited interpreter/translator with the Immigration and Refugee Board of Canada and the Ministry of the Attorney General for the last thirty years. She has been an Expert Witness in the field of social and cultural conditions of Bangladesh, for the Supreme Court of St. John's, Newfoundland, Canada, since 1997.

She currently resides in Mississauga, Ontario, Canada.

To learn more about Rummana and her work, visit her website or connect with her on social media.

www.rummanachowdhury.com
Instagram: @rummanachowdhury
Facebook: Rummana Chowdhury